Jules Verne

The Pearl of Lima

I0599269

Outlook

Jules Verne

The Pearl of Lima

1. Auflage | ISBN: 978-3-73262-399-0

Erscheinungsort: Frankfurt am Main, Deutschland

Erscheinungsjahr: 2018

Outlook Verlag GmbH, Frankfurt.

Jules Verne

The Pearl of Lima

Outlook

THE PEARL OF LIMA.
BY ANNE T. WILBUR.
Graham's American Monthly Magazine of Literature, Art, and Fashion (1844-1858); Apr 1853; VOL. XLII., No. 4; APS pg. 422

THE PEARL OF LIMA.

A STORY OF TRUE LOVE.

TRANSLATED FROM THE FRENCH OF M. JULES VERNE.

BY ANNE T. WILBUR.

Transcriber's Note: Minor typographical errors have been corrected without note. Inconsistent hyphenation and spellings have been standardised, whilst variant and unique spellings remain as printed. For the reader's ease, although not present in the original text, a brief table of contents has been included below:

CHAPTER I.

THE PLAZA-MAYOR.

The sun had disappeared behind the snowy peaks of the Cordilleras; but the beautiful Peruvian sky long retains, through the transparent veil of night, the reflection of his rays; the atmosphere is impregnated with a refreshing coolness, which in these burning latitudes affords freedom of breath; it is the hour in which one can live a European life, and seek without on the verandas some cooling gentle zephyr; it seems as if a metallic roof was then interposed between the sun and the earth, which, retaining the heat and suffering only the light to pass, offers beneath its shelter a reparative repose.

This much desired hour had at last sounded from the clock of the cathedral. While the earliest stars were rising above the horizon, the numerous promenaders were traversing the streets of Lima, wrapped in their light mantles, and conversing gravely on the most trivial affairs. There was a great movement of the populace on the Plaza-Mayor, that forum of the ancient city of kings; artisans were profiting by the coolness to quit their daily labors; they circulated actively among the crowd, crying their various merchandise; the ladies of Lima, carefully enveloped in the mantillas which mask their countenances, with the exception of the right eye, darted stealthy glances on the surrounding masses; they undulated through the groups of smokers, like foam at the will of the waves; other señoras, in ball costume, *coiffed* only with their abundant hair or some natural flowers, passed in large calêches, throwing on the *caballeros* nonchalant regards.

But these glances were not bestowed indiscriminately upon the young cavaliers; the thoughts of the noble ladies could rest only on aristocratic heights. The Indians passed without lifting their eyes upon them, knowing themselves to be beneath their notice; betraying by no gesture or word, the bitter envy of their hearts. They contrasted strongly with the half-breeds, or mestizoes, who, repulsed like the former, vented their indignation in cries and protestations.

The proud descendants of Pizarro marched with heads high, as in the times when their ancestors founded the city of kings; their traditional scorn rested alike on the Indians whom they had conquered, and the mestizoes, born of their relations with the natives of the New World. The Indians, on the contrary, were constantly struggling to break their chains, and cherished alike aversion toward the conquerors of the ancient empire of the Incas and their haughty and insolent descendants.

But the mestizoes, Spanish in their contempt for the Indians, and Indian in their hatred which they had vowed against the Spaniards, burned with both these vivid and impassioned sentiments.

A group of these young people stood near the pretty fountain in the centre of the Plaza-Mayor. Clad in their *poncho*, a piece of cloth or cotton in the form of a parallelogram, with an opening in the middle to give passage to the head, in large pantaloons, striped with a thousand colors, *coiffed* with broad-brimmed hats of Guayaquil straw, they were talking, declaiming, gesticulating.

"You are right, André," said a very obsequious young man, whom they called Milleflores.

This was the friend, the parasite of André Certa, a young mestizo of swarthy complexion, whose thin beard gave a singular appearance to his countenance.

André Certa, the son of a rich merchant killed in the last *émeute* of the conspirator Lafuente, had inherited a large fortune; this he freely scattered among his friends, whose humble salutations he demanded in exchange for handfuls of gold.

"Of what use are these changes in government, these eternal *pronunciamentos* which disturb Peru to gratify private ambition?" resumed André, in a loud voice; "what is it to me whether Gambarra or Santa Cruz rule, if there is no equality."

"Well said," exclaimed Milleflores, who, under the most republican government, could never have been the equal of a man of sense.

"How is it," resumed André Certa, "that I, the son of a merchant, can ride only in a calêche drawn by mules? Have not my ships brought wealth and prosperity to the country? Is not the aristocracy of piasters worth all the titles of Spain?"

"It is a shame!" resumed the young mestizo. "There is Don Fernand, who passes in his carriage drawn by two horses! Don Fernand d'Aiquillo! He has scarcely property enough to feed his coachman and horses, and he must come to parade himself proudly about the square. And, hold! here is another! the Marquis Don Vegal!"

A magnificent carriage, drawn by four fine horses, at that moment entered the Plaza-Mayor; its only occupant was a man of proud mien, mingled with sadness; he gazed, without seeming to see them, on the multitude assembled to breathe the coolness of the evening. This man was the Marquis Don Vegal, knight of Alcantara, of Malta, and of Charles III. He had a right to appear in this pompous equipage; the viceroy and the archbishop could alone take

5

precedence of him; but this great nobleman came here from ennui and not from ostentation; his thoughts were not depicted on his countenance, they were concentrated beneath his bent brow; he received no impression from exterior objects, on which he bestowed not a look, and heard not the envious reflections of the mestizoes, when his four horses made their way through the crowd.

"I hate that man," said André Certa.

"You will not hate him long."

"I know it! All these nobles are displaying the last splendors of their luxury; I can tell where their silver and their family jewels go."

"You have not your entrée with the Jew Samuel for nothing."

"Certainly not! On his account-books are inscribed aristocratic creditors; in his strong-box are piled the wrecks of great fortunes; and in the day when the Spaniards shall be as ragged as their Cæsar de Bazan, we will have fine sport."

"Yes, we will have fine sport, dear André, mounted on your millions, on a golden pedestal! And you are about to double your fortune! When are you to marry the beautiful young daughter of old Samuel, a Limanienne to the end of her nails, with nothing Jewish about her but her name of Sarah?"

"In a month," replied André Certa, proudly, "there will be no fortune in Peru which can compete with mine."

"But why," asked some one, "do you not espouse some Spanish girl of high descent?"

"I despise these people as much as I hate them."

André Certa concealed the fact of his having been repulsed by several noble families, into which he had sought to introduce himself.

His interlocutor still wore an expression of doubt, and the brow of the mestizo had contracted, when the latter was rudely elbowed by a man of tall stature, whose gray hairs proclaimed him to be at least fifty, while the muscular force of his firmly knit limbs seemed undiminished by age.

This man was clad in a brown vest, through which appeared a coarse shirt with a broad collar; his short breeches, striped with green, were fastened by red garters to stockings of clay-color; on his feet were sandals made of *ojotas*, ox-hide prepared for this purpose; beneath his high-pointed hat gleamed large ear-rings. His complexion was dark. After having jostled André Certa, he looked at him fixedly, but with no particular expression.

"Miserable Indian!" exclaimed the mestizo, raising his hand upon him.

His companions restrained him. Milleflores, whose face was pale with terror, exclaimed:

"André! André! take care."

"A vile slave! to presume to elbow me!"

"It is a madman! it is the *Sambo*!"

The *Sambo*, as the name indicated, was an Indian of the mountains; he continued to fix his eyes on the mestizo, whom he had intentionally jostled. The latter, whose anger was unbounded, had seized a poignard at his girdle, and was about to have rushed on the impassable aggressor, when a guttural cry, like that of the *cilguero*, (a kind of linnet of Peru,) re-echoed in the midst of the tumult of promenaders, and the Sambo disappeared.

"Brutal and cowardly!" exclaimed André.

"Control yourself," said Milleflores, softly. "Let us leave the Plaza-Mayor; the Limanienne ladies are too haughty here."

As he said these words, the brave Milleflores looked cautiously around to see whether he was not within reach of the foot or arm of some Indian in the neighborhood.

"In an hour, I must be at the house of Jew Samuel," said André.

"In an hour! we have time to pass to the *Calle del Peligro*; you can offer some oranges or ananas to the charming *tapadas* who promenade there. Shall we go, gentlemen?"

The group directed their steps toward the extremity of the square, and began to descend the street of Danger, where Milleflores hoped his good looks would be appreciated; but it was nightfall, and the young Limaniennes merited better than ever their name of *tapadas* (hidden), for they drew their mantles more closely over their countenances.

The Plaza-Mayor was all alive; the cries and the tumult were redoubled; the guards on horseback, stationed before the central portico of the viceroy's palace, situated on the north side of the square, could scarcely maintain their position amid the shifting crowd; there were merchants for all customers and customers for all merchants. The greatest variety of trades seemed to be congregated there, and from the *Portal de Escribanos* to the *Portal de Botoneros*, there was one immense display of articles of every kind, the Plaza-Mayor serving at once as promenade, bazaar, market and fair. The ground-floor of the viceroy's palace is occupied by shops; along the first story runs an immense gallery where the crowd can promenade on days of public rejoicing;

on the east side of the square rises the cathedral, with its steeples and light balustrades, proudly adorning its two towers; the basement story of the edifice being ten feet high, and containing warehouses full of the products of tropical climates.

In the centre of this square is situated the beautiful fountain, constructed in 1653, by the orders of the viceroy, the Comte de Salvatierra. From the top of the pillar, which rises in the middle of the fountain and is surmounted with a statue of Fame, the water falls in sheets, and is discharged into a basin beneath through the mouths of lions. It is here that the water-carriers (*aguadores*) load their mules with barrels, attach a bell to a hoop, and mount behind their liquid merchandise.

This square is therefore noisy from morning till evening, and when the stars of night rise above the snowy summits of the Cordilleras, the tumult of the *élite* of Lima equals the matinal hubbub of the merchants.

Nevertheless, when the *oracion* (evening *angelus*) sounds from the bell of the cathedral, all this noise suddenly ceases; to the clamor of pleasure succeeds the murmur of prayer; the women pause in their walk and put their hands on their rosaries, invoking the Virgin Mary. Then, not a merchant dares sell his merchandise, not a customer thinks of buying, and this square, so recently animated, seems to have become a vast solitude.

While the Limanians paused and knelt at the sound of the *angelus*, a young girl, carefully surrounded by her discreet mantle, sought to pass through the praying multitude; she was followed by a mestizo woman, a sort of duenna, who watched every glance and step. The duenna, as if she had not understood the warning bell, continued her way through the devout populace: to the general surprise succeeded harsh epithets. The young girl would have stopped, but the duenna kept on.

"Do you see that daughter of Satan?" said some one near her.

"Who is that *balarina*—that impious dancer?"

"It is one of the Carcaman women." (A reproachful name bestowed upon Europeans.)

The young girl at last stopped, blushing and confused.

Suddenly a *gaucho*, a merchant of mules, seized her by the shoulder, and would have compelled her to kneel; but he had scarcely laid his hand upon her when a vigorous arm rudely felled him to the ground. This scene, rapid as lightning, was followed by a moment of confusion.

"Save yourself, miss," said a gentle and respectful voice in the ear of the young girl.

The latter turned, pale with terror, and saw a young Indian of tall stature, who, with his arms tranquilly folded, was awaiting with firm foot the attack of his adversary.

"We are lost!" exclaimed the duenna; "*niña, niña*, let us go, for the love of God!" and she seized the arm of the young girl who disappeared, while the crowd rose and dispersed.

The *gaucho* had risen, bruised with his fall, and thinking it not prudent to seek revenge, rejoined his mules, muttering threats.

CHAPTER II.

EVENING IN THE STREETS OF LIMA.

Night had succeeded, almost without intervening twilight, the glare of day. The two women quickened their pace, for it was late: the young girl, still under the influence of strong emotion, maintained silence, while the duenna murmured some mysterious paternosters—they walked rapidly through one of the sloping streets leading from the Plaza-Mayor.

This place is situated more than four hundred feet above the level of the sea, and about a hundred and fifty rods from the bridge thrown over the river Rimac, which forms the diameter of the city of Lima, arranged in a semicircle.

The city of Lima lies in the valley of the Rimac, nine leagues from its mouth; at the north and east commence the first undulations of ground which form a part of the great chain of the Andes: the valley of Lungaucho, formed by the mountains of San Cristoval and the Amancaes, which rise behind Lima, terminates in its suburbs. The city lies on one bank of the river; the other is occupied by the suburb of San Lazaro, and is united to the city by a bridge of five arches, the upper piers of which are triangular to break the force of the current; while the lower ones present to the promenaders circular benches, on which the fashionables may lounge during the summer evenings, and where they can contemplate a pretty cascade.

The city is two miles long from east to west, and only a mile and a quarter wide from the bridge to the walls; the latter, twelve feet in height, ten feet thick at their base, are built of *adobes*, a kind of brick dried in the sun, and made of potter's clay mingled with a great quantity of chopped straw: these walls are calculated to resist earthquakes; the enclosure, pierced with seven gates and three posterns, terminates at its south-east extremity by the little citadel of Santa Caterina.

Such is the ancient city of kings, founded in 1534 by Pizarro, on the day of Epiphany; it has been and is still the theatre of constantly renewed revolutions. Lima, situated three miles from the sea, was formerly the principal storehouse of America on the Pacific Ocean, thanks to its Port of Callao, built in 1779, in a singular manner. An old vessel, filled with stones, sand, and rubbish of all sorts, was wrecked on the shore; piles of the mangrove-tree, brought from Guayaquil and impervious to water, were driven around this as a centre, which became the immovable base on which rose the mole of Callao.

The climate, milder and more temperate than that of Carthagena or Bahia, situated on the opposite side of America, makes Lima one of the most agreeable cities of the New World: the wind has two directions from which it never varies; either it blows from the south-east, and becomes cool by crossing the Pacific Ocean; or it comes from the south-west, impregnated with the mild atmosphere of the forests and the freshness which it has derived from the icy summits of the Cordilleras.

The nights beneath tropical latitudes are very beautiful and very clear; they mysteriously prepare that beneficent dew which fertilizes a soil exposed to the rays of a cloudless sky—so the inhabitants of Lima prolong their nocturnal conversations and receptions; household labors are quietly finished in the dwellings refreshed by the shadows, and the streets are soon deserted; scarcely is some *pulperia* still haunted by the drinkers of *chica* or *quarapo*.

These, the young girl, whom we have seen, carefully avoided; crossing in the middle of the numerous squares scattered about the city, she arrived, without interruption, at the bridge of the Rimac, listening to catch the slightest sound —which her emotion exaggerated, and hearing only the bells of a train of mules conducted by its *arriero*, or the joyous *stribillo* of some Indian.

This young girl was called Sarah, and was returning to the house of the Jew Samuel, her father; she was clad in a *saya* of satin—a kind of petticoat of a dark color, plaited in elastic folds, and very narrow at the bottom, which compelled her to take short steps, and gave her that graceful delicacy peculiar to the Limanienne ladies; this petticoat, ornamented with lace and flowers, was in part covered with a silk mantle, which was raised above the head and enveloped it like a hood; stockings of exquisite fineness and little satin shoes peeped out beneath the graceful *saya*; bracelets of great value encircled the arms of the young girl, whose rich toilet was of exquisite taste, and her whole person redolent of that charm so well expressed by the Spanish word *donaire*.

Milleflores might well say to André Certa that his betrothed had nothing of the Jewess but the name, for she was a faithful specimen of those admirable señoras whose beauty is above all praise.

The duenna, an old Jewess, whose countenance was expressive of avarice and cupidity, was a devoted servant of Samuel, who paid her liberally.

At the moment when these two women entered the suburb of San Lazaro, a man, clad in the robe of a monk, and with his head covered with a cowl, passed near them and looked at them attentively. This man, of tall stature, possessed a countenance expressive of gentleness and benevolence; it was Padre Joachim de Camarones; he threw a glance of intelligence on Sarah, who immediately looked at her follower.

The latter was still grumbling, muttering and whining, which prevented her seeing any thing; the young girl turned toward the good father and made a graceful sign with her hand.

"Well, señora," said the old woman, sharply, "is it not enough to have been insulted by these Christians, that you should stop to look at a priest?"

Sarah did not reply.

"Shall we see you one day, with rosary in hand, engaged in the ceremonies of the church?"

The ceremonies of the church—*las funciones de iglesia*—are the great business of the Limanian ladies.

"You make strange suppositions," replied the young girl, blushing.

"Strange as your conduct! What would my master Samuel say, if he knew what had taken place this evening?"

"Am I to blame because a brutal muleteer chose to address me?"

"I understand, señora," said the old woman, shaking her head, "and will not speak of the *gaucho*."

"Then the young man did wrong in defending me from the abuse of the populace?"

"Is it the first time the Indian has thrown himself in your way?"

The countenance of the young girl was fortunately sheltered by her mantle, for the darkness would not have sufficed to conceal her emotion from the inquisitive glance of the duenna.

"But let us leave the Indian where he is," resumed the old woman, "it is not my business to watch him. What I complain of is, that in order not to disturb these Christians, you wished to remain among them! Had you not some desire to kneel with them? Ah, señora, your father would soon dismiss me if I were guilty of such apostasy."

But the young girl no longer heard; the remark of the old woman on the subject of the young Indian had inspired her with sweeter thoughts; it seemed to her that the intervention of this young man was providential; and she turned several times to see if he had not followed her in the shadow. Sarah had in her heart a certain natural confidence which became her wonderfully; she felt herself to be the child of these warm latitudes, which the sun decorates with surprising vegetation; proud as a Spaniard, if she had fixed her regards on this man, it was because he had stood proudly in the presence of her pride, and had not begged a glance as a reward of his protection.

In imagining that the Indian was near her, Sarah was not mistaken; Martin Paz, after having come to the assistance of the young girl, wished to ensure her safe retreat; so when the promenaders had dispersed, he followed her, without being perceived by her, but without concealing himself; the darkness alone favoring his pursuit.

This Martin Paz was a handsome young man, wearing with unparalleled nobility the national costume of the Indian of the mountains; from his broad-brimmed straw hat escaped fine black hair, whose curls harmonized with the bronze of his manly face. His eyes shone with infinite sweetness, like the transparent atmosphere of starry nights; his well-formed nose surmounted a pretty mouth, unlike that of most of his race. He was one of the noblest descendants of Manco-Capac, and his veins were full of that ardent blood which leads men to the accomplishment of lofty deeds.

He was proudly draped in his *poncho* of brilliant colors; at his girdle hung one of those Malay poignards, so terrible in a practiced hand, for they seem to be riveted to the arm which strikes. In North America, on the shores of Lake Ontario, Martin Paz would have been a great chief among those wandering tribes which have fought with the English so many heroic combats.

Martin Paz knew that Sarah was the daughter of the wealthy Samuel; he knew her to be the most charming woman in Lima; he knew her to be betrothed to the opulent mestizo André Certa; he knew that by her birth, her position and her wealth she was beyond the reach of his heart; but he forgot all these impossibilities in his all-absorbing passion. It seemed to him that this beautiful young girl belonged to him, as the llama to the Peruvian forests, as the eagle to the depths of immensity.

Plunged in his reflections, Martin Paz hastened his steps to see the *saya* of the young girl sweep the threshold of the paternal dwelling; and Sarah herself, half-opening then her mantilla, cast on him a bewildering glance of gratitude.

He was quickly joined by two Indians of the species of *zambos*, pillagers and robbers, who walked beside him.

"Martin Paz," said one of them to him, "you ought this very evening to meet our brethren in the mountains."

"I shall be there," coldly replied the other.

"The schooner *Annonciation* has appeared in sight from Callao, tacked for a few moments, then, protected by the point, rapidly disappeared. She will undoubtedly approach the land near the mouth of the Rimac, and our bark canoes must be there to relieve her of her merchandise. We shall need your presence."

"You are losing time by your observations. Martin Paz knows his duty and he will do it."

"It is in the name of the Sambo that we speak to you here."

"It is in my own name that I speak to you."

"Do you not fear that he will find your presence in the suburb of San Lazaro at this hour unaccountable?"

"I am where my fancy and my will have brought me."

"Before the house of the Jew?"

"Those of my brethren who are disposed to find fault can meet me to-night in the mountain."

The eyes of the three men sparkled, and this was all. The *zambos* regained the bank of the Rimac, and the sound of their footsteps died away in the darkness.

Martin Paz had hastily approached the house of the Jew. This house, like all those of Lima, had but two stories; the ground floor, built of bricks, was surmounted with walls formed of canes tied together and covered with plaster; all this part of the building, constructed to resist earthquakes, imitated, by a skillful painting, the bricks of the lower story; the square roof, called *asoetas*, was covered with flowers, and formed a terrace full of perfumes and pretty points of view.

A vast gate, placed between two pavilions, gave access to a court; but as usual, these pavilions had no window opening upon the street.

The clock of the parish church was striking eleven when Martin Paz stopped before the dwelling of Sarah. Profound silence reigned around; a flickering light within proved that the saloon of the Jew Samuel was still occupied.

Why does the Indian stand motionless before these silent walls? The cool atmosphere woos him with its transparency and its perfumes; the radiant stars send down upon the sleeping earth rays of diaphanous mildness; the white constellations illumine the darkness with their enchanting light; his heart believes in those sympathetic communications which brave time and distance.

A white form appears upon the terrace amid the flowers to which night has only left a vague outline, without diminishing their delicious perfumes; the dahlias mingle with the mentzelias, with the helianthus, and, beneath the occidental breeze, form a waving basket which surrounds Sarah, the young and beautiful Jewess.

Martin Paz involuntarily raises his hands and clasps them with adoration.

15

Suddenly the white form sinks down, as if terrified.

Martin Paz turns, and finds himself face to face with André Certa.

"Since when do the Indians pass their nights in contemplation?"

André Certa spoke angrily.

"Since the Indians have trodden the soil of their ancestors."

"Have they no longer, on the mountain side, some *yaravis* to chant, some *boleros* to dance with the girls of their caste?"

"The *cholos*," replied the Indian, in a high voice, "bestow their devotion where it is merited; the Indians love according to their hearts."

André Certa became pale with anger; he advanced a step toward his immovable rival.

"Wretch! will you quit this place?"

"Rather quit it yourself," shouted Martin Paz; and two poignards gleamed in the two right hands of the adversaries; they were of equal stature, they seemed of equal strength, and the lightnings of their eyes were reflected in the steel of their arms.

André Certa rapidly raised his arm, which he dropped still more quickly. But his poignard had encountered the Malay poignard of the Indian; at the fire which flashed from this shock, André saw the arm of Martin Paz suspended over his head, and immediately rolled on the earth, his arm pierced through.

"Help, help!" he exclaimed.

The door of the Jew's house opened at his cries. Some mestizoes ran from a neighboring house; some pursued the Indian, who fled rapidly; others raised the wounded man. He had swooned.

"Who is this man?" said one of them. "If he is a sailor, take him to the hospital of Spiritu Santo; if an Indian, to the hospital of Santa Anna."

An old man advanced toward the wounded youth; he had scarcely looked upon him when he exclaimed:

"Let the poor young man be carried into my house. This is a strange mischance."

This man was the Jew Samuel; he had just recognized the betrothed of his daughter.

Martin Paz, thanks to the darkness and the rapidity of his flight, may hope to escape his pursuers; he has risked his life; an Indian assassin of a mestizo! If he can gain the open country he is safe, but he knows that the gates of the city are closed at eleven o'clock in the evening, not to be re-opened till four in the morning.

He reaches at last the stone bridge which he had already crossed. The Indians, and some soldiers who had joined them, pursue him closely; he springs upon the bridge. Unfortunately a patrol appears at the opposite extremity; Martin Paz can neither advance nor retrace his steps; without hesitation he clears the parapet and leaps into the rapid current which breaks against the corners of the stones.

The pursuers spring upon the banks below the bridge to seize the swimmer at his landing.

But it is in vain; Martin Paz does not re-appear.

CHAPTER III.

THE JEW EVERY WHERE A JEW.

André Certa, once introduced into the house of Samuel, and laid in a bed hastily prepared, recovered his senses and pressed the hand of the old Jew. The physician, summoned by one of the domestics, was promptly in attendance. The wound appeared to be a slight one; the shoulder of the mestizo had been pierced in such a manner that the steel had only glided among the flesh. In a few days, André Certa might be once more upon his feet.

When Samuel was left alone with André, the latter said to him:

"You would do well to wall up the gate which leads to your terrace, Master Samuel."

"What fear you, André?"

"I fear lest Sarah should present herself there to the contemplation of the Indians. It was not a robber who attacked me; it was a rival, from whom I have escaped but by miracle!"

"By the holy tables, it is a task to bring up young girls!" exclaimed the Jew. "But you are mistaken, señor," he resumed, "Sarah will be a dutiful spouse. I spare no pains that she may do you honor."

André Certa half raised himself on his elbow.

"Master Samuel, there is one thing which you do not enough remember, that I pay you for the hand of Sarah a hundred thousand piasters."

"Señor," replied the Jew, with a miserly chuckle, "I remember it so well, that I am ready now to exchange this receipt for the money."

As he said this, Samuel drew from his pocket-book a paper which André Certa repulsed with his hand.

"The bargain is not complete until Sarah has become my wife, and she will never be such if her hand is to be disputed by such an adversary. You know, Master Samuel, what is my object; in espousing Sarah, I wish to be the equal of this nobility which casts such scornful glances upon us."

"And you will, señor, for you see the proudest grandees of Spain throng our saloons, around the pearl of Lima."

"Where has Sarah been this evening?"

"To the Israelitish temple, with old Ammon."

"Why should Sarah attend your religious rites?"

"I am a Jew, señor," replied Samuel proudly, "and would Sarah be my daughter if she did not fulfill the duties of my religion?"

The old Jew remained sad and silent for several minutes. His bent brow rested on one of his withered hands. His face usually bronze, was now almost pale; beneath a brown cap appeared locks of an indescribable color. He was clad in a sort of great-coat fastened around the waist.

This old man trafficked every where and in every thing; he might have been a descendant of the Judas who sold his Master for thirty pieces of silver. He had been a resident of Lima ten years; his taste and his economy had led him to choose his dwelling at the extremity of the suburb of San Lazaro, and from thence he entered into various speculations to make money. By degrees, Samuel assumed a luxury uncommon in misers; his house was sumptuously furnished; his numerous domestics, his splendid equipages betokened immense revenues. Sarah was then eight years of age. Already graceful and charming, she pleased all, and was the idol of the Jew. All her inclinations were unhesitatingly gratified. Always elegantly dressed, she attracted the eyes of the most fastidious, of which her father seemed strangely careless. It will readily be understood how the mestizo, André Certa, became enamored of the beautiful Jewess. What would have appeared inexplicable to the public, was the hundred thousand piasters, the price of her hand; but this bargain was secret. And besides, Samuel trafficked in sentiments as in native productions. A banker, usurer, merchant, ship-owner, he had the talent to do business with everybody. The schooner *Annonciation*, which was hovering about the mouth of the Rimac, belonged to the Jew Samuel.

Amid this life of business and speculation this man fulfilled the duties of his religion with scrupulous punctuality; his daughter had been carefully instructed in the Israelitish faith and practices.

So, when the mestizo had manifested his displeasure on this subject, the old man remained mute and pensive, and André Certa broke the silence, saying:

"Do you forget that the motive for which I espouse Sarah will compel her to become a convert to Catholicism? It is not my fault," added the mestizo; "but in spite of you, in spite of me, in spite of herself, it will be so."

"You are right," said the Jew sadly; "but, by the Bible, Sarah shall be a Jewess as long as she is my daughter."

At this moment the door of the chamber opened, and the major-domo of the Jew Samuel respectfully entered.

"Is the murderer arrested?" asked the old man.

"We have reason to believe he is dead!"

"Dead!" repeated André, with a joyful exclamation.

"Caught between us and a company of soldiers," replied the major-domo, "he was obliged to leap over the parapet of the bridge."

"He has thrown himself into the Rimac!" exclaimed André.

"And how do you know that he has not reached the shore?" asked Samuel.

"The melting of the snow has made the current rapid at that spot; besides, we stationed ourselves on each side of the river, and he did not re-appear. I have left sentinels who will pass the night in watching the banks."

"It is well," said the old man; "he has met with a just fate. Did you recognize him in his flight?"

"Perfectly, sir; it was Martin Paz, the Indian of the mountains."

"Has this man been observing Sarah for some time past?"

"I do not know," replied the servant.

"Summon old Ammon."

The major-domo withdrew.

"These Indians," said the old man, "have secret understandings among themselves; I must know whether the pursuit of this man dates from a distant period."

The duenna entered, and remained standing before her master.

"Does my daughter," asked Samuel, "know any thing of what has taken place this morning?"

"When the cries of your servants awoke me, I ran to the chamber of the señora, and found her almost motionless and of a mortal paleness."

"Fatality!" said Samuel; "continue," added he, seeing that the mestizo was apparently asleep.

"To my urgent inquiries as to the cause of her agitation, the señora would not reply; she retired without accepting my services, and I withdrew."

"Has this Indian often thrown himself in her way?"

"I do not know, master; nevertheless I have often met him in the streets of San Lazaro."

"And you have told me nothing of this?"

21

"He came to her assistance this evening on the Plaza-Mayor," added the old duenna.

"Her assistance! how?"

The old woman related the scene with downcast head.

"Ah! my daughter wish to kneel among these Christians!" exclaimed the Jew, angrily; "and I knew nothing of all this! You deserve that I should dismiss you."

The duenna went out of the room in confusion.

"Do you not see that the marriage should take place soon?" said André Certa. "I am not asleep, Master Samuel! But I need rest, now, and I will dream of our espousals."

At these words, the old man slowly retired. Before regaining his room, he wished to assure himself of the condition of his daughter, and softly entered the chamber of Sarah.

The young girl was in an agitated slumber, in the midst of the rich silk drapery around her; a watch-lamp of alabaster, suspended from the arabesques of the ceiling, shed its soft light upon her beautiful countenance; the half-open window admitted, through lowered blinds, the quiet coolness of the air, impregnated with the penetrating perfumes of the aloes and magnolia; creole luxury was displayed in the thousand objects of art which good taste and grace had dispersed on richly carved *étagères*; and, beneath the vague and placid rays of night, it seemed as if the soul of the child was sporting amid these wonders.

The old man approached the bed of Sarah: he bent over her to listen. The beautiful Jewess seemed disturbed by sorrowful thoughts, and more than once the name of Martin Paz escaped her lips.

Samuel regained his chamber, uttering maledictions.

At the first rays of morning, Sarah hastily arose. Liberta, a full-blooded Indian attached to her service, hastened to her; and, in pursuance of her orders, saddled a mule for his mistress and a horse for himself.

Sarah was accustomed to take morning-rides, accompanied by this Indian, who was entirely devoted to her.

She was clad in a *saya* of a brown color, and a mantle of cashmere with long tassels; her head was not covered with the usual hood, but sheltered beneath the broad brim of a straw hat, which left her long black tresses to float over her shoulders; and to conceal any unusual pre-occupation, she held between her lips a *cigarette* of perfumed tobacco.

Liberta, clad like an Indian of the mountains, prepared to accompany his mistress.

"Liberta," said the young girl to him, "remember to be blind and dumb."

Once in the saddle, Sarah left the city as usual, and began to ride through the country; she directed her way toward Callao. The port was in full animation: there had been a conflict during the night between the revenue-officers and a schooner, whose undecided movements betrayed a fraudulent speculation. The *Annonciation* seemed to have been awaiting some suspicious barks near the mouth of the Rimac; but before the latter could reach her, she had been compelled to flee before the custom-house boats, which had boldly given her chase.

Various rumors were in circulation respecting the destination of this vessel—which bore no name on her stern. According to some, this schooner, laden with Colombian troops, was seeking to seize the principal vessels of Callao; for Bolivar had it in his heart to revenge the affront given to the soldiers left by him in Peru, and who had been driven from it in disgrace.

According to others, the schooner was simply a smuggler of European goods.

Without troubling herself about these rumors, more or less important, Sarah, whose ride to the port had been only a pretext, returned toward Lima, which she reached near the banks of the Rimac.

She ascended them toward the bridge: numbers of soldiers, mestizoes, and Indians, were stationed at various points on the shore.

Liberta had acquainted the young girl with the events of the night. In compliance with her orders, he interrogated some Indians leaning over the parapet, and learned that although Martin Paz had been undoubtedly drowned, his body had not yet been recovered.

Sarah was pale and almost fainting; it required all her strength of soul not to abandon herself to her grief.

Among the people wandering on the banks, she remarked an Indian with ferocious features—the Sambo! He was crouched on the bank, and seemed a prey to despair.

As Sarah passed near the old mountaineer, she heard these words, full of gloomy anger:

"Wo! wo! They have killed the son of the Sambo! They have killed my son!"

The young girl resolutely drew herself up, made a sign to Liberta to follow her; and this time, without caring whether she was observed or not, went directly to the church of Santa Anna; left her mule in charge of the Indian, entered the Catholic temple, and asking for the good Father Joachim, knelt on the stone steps, praying to Jesus and Mary for the soul of Martin Paz.

CHAPTER IV.
A SPANISH GRANDEE.

Any other than the Indian, Martin Paz, would have, indeed, perished in the waters of the Rimac; to escape death, his surprising strength, his insurmountable will, and especially his sublime coolness, one of the privileges of the free hordes of the *pampas* of the New World, had all been found necessary.

Martin knew that his pursuers would concentrate their efforts to seize him below the bridge; it seemed impossible for him to overcome the current, and that the Indian must be carried down; but by vigorous strokes he succeeded in stemming the torrent; he dived repeatedly, and finding the under-currents less strong, at last ventured to land, and concealed himself behind a thicket of mangrove-trees.

But what was to become of him? Retreat was perilous; the soldiers might change their plans and ascend the river; the Indian must then inevitably be captured; he would lose his life, and, worse yet, Sarah. His decision was rapidly made; through the narrow streets and deserted squares he plunged into the heart of the city; but it was important that he should be supposed dead; he therefore avoided being seen, since his garments, dripping with water and covered with sea-weed, would have betrayed him.

To avoid the indiscreet glances of some belated inhabitants, Martin Paz was obliged to pass through one of the widest streets of the city; a house still brilliantly illuminated presented itself: the *port-cochere* was open to give passage to the elegant equipages which were issuing from the court, and conveying to their respective dwellings the nobles of the Spanish aristocracy.

The Indian adroitly glided into this magnificent dwelling; he could not remain in the street, where curious *zambos* were thronging around, attracted by the carriages. The gates of the hotel were soon carefully closed, and the Indian found flight impossible.

Some lacqueys were going to and fro in the court; Martin Paz rapidly passed up a rich stairway of cedar-wood, ornamented with valuable tapestry; the saloons, still illuminated, presented no convenient place of refuge; he crossed them with the rapidity of lightning, and disappeared in a room filled with protecting darkness.

The last lustres were quickly extinguished, and the house became profoundly silent.

The Indian Paz, as a man of energy to whom moments are precious, hastened to reconnoitre the place, and to find the surest means of evasion; the windows of this chamber opened on an interior garden; flight was practicable, and Martin Paz was about to spring from them, when he heard these words:

"Señor, you have forgotten to take the diamonds which I had left on that table!"

Martin Paz turned. A man of noble stature and of great pride of countenance was pointing to a jewel-case.

At this insult Martin Paz laid his hand on his poignard. He approached the Spaniard, who stood unmoved, and, in a first impulse of indignation, raised his arm to strike him; but turning his weapon against himself, said, in a deep tone,

"Señor, if you repeat such words, I will kill myself at your feet."

The Spaniard, astonished, looked at the Indian more attentively, and through his tangled and dripping locks perceived so lofty a frankness, that he felt a strange sympathy fill his heart. He went toward the window, gently closed it, and returned toward the Indian, whose poignard had fallen to the ground.

"Who are you?" said he to him.

"The Indian, Martin Paz. I am pursued by soldiers for having defended myself against a mestizo who attacked me, and levelled him to the ground with a blow from my poignard. This mestizo is the betrothed of a young girl whom I love. Now, señor, you can deliver me to my enemies, if you judge it noble and right."

"Sir," replied the Spaniard, gravely, "I depart to-morrow for the Baths of Chorillos; if you please to accompany me, you will be for the present safe from pursuit, and will never have reason to complain of the hospitality of the Marquis Don Vegal."

Martin Paz bent coldly without manifesting any emotion.

"You can rest until morning on this bed," resumed Don Vegal; "no one here will suspect your retreat. Good-night, señor!"

The Spaniard went out of the room, and left the Indian, moved to tears by a confidence so generous; he yielded himself entirely to the protection of the marquis, and without thinking that his slumbers might be taken advantage of to seize him, slept with peaceful security.

The next day, at sunrise, the marquis gave the last orders for his departure, and summoned the Jew Samuel to come to him; in the meantime he attended the morning mass.

This was a custom generally observed by the aristocracy. From its very foundation Lima had been essentially Catholic. Besides its numerous churches, it numbered twenty-two convents, seventeen monasteries, and four *beaterios*, or houses of retreat for females who did not take the vows. Each of these establishments possessed a chapel, so that there were at Lima more than a hundred edifices for worship, where eight hundred secular or regular priests, three hundred *religieuses*, lay-brothers and sisters, performed the duties of religion.

As Don Vegal entered the church of Santa Anna, he noticed a young girl kneeling in prayer and in tears. There was so much of grief in her depression, that the marquis could not look at her without emotion; and he was preparing to console her by some kind words, when Father Joachim de Camarones approached him, saying in a low voice:

"Señor Don Vegal, pray do not approach her."

Then he made a sign to Sarah, who followed him to an obscure and deserted chapel.

Don Vegal directed his steps to the altar and listened to the mass; then, as he was returning, he thought involuntarily of the deep sadness of the kneeling maiden. Her image followed him to his hotel, and remained deeply engraven in his soul.

Don Vegal found in his saloon the Jew Samuel, who had come in compliance with his request. Samuel seemed to have forgotten the events of the night; the hope of gain animated his countenance with a natural gayety.

"What is your lordship's will?" asked he of the Spaniard.

"I must have thirty thousand piasters within an hour."

"Thirty thousand piasters! And who has them! By the holy king David, my lord, I am far from being able to furnish such a sum."

"Here are some jewels of great value," resumed Don Vegal, without noticing the language of the Jew; "besides I can sell you at a low price a considerable estate near Cusco."

"Ah! señor, lands ruin us—we have not arms enough left to cultivate them; the Indians have withdrawn to the mountains, and our harvests do not pay us for the trouble they cost."

"At what value do you estimate these diamonds?"

Samuel drew from his pocket a little pair of scales and began to weigh the stones with scrupulous skill. As he did this, he continued to talk, and, as was his custom, depreciated the pledges offered him.

"Diamonds! a poor investment! What would they bring? One might as well bury money! You will notice, señor, that this is not of the purest water. Do you know that I do not find a ready market for these costly ornaments? I am obliged to send such merchandise to the United Provinces! The Americans would buy them, undoubtedly, but to give them up to the sons of Albion. They wish besides, and it is very just, to gain an honest per centage, so that the depreciation falls upon me. I think that ten thousand piasters should satisfy your lordship. It is little, I know; but——"

"Have I not said," resumed the Spaniard, with a sovereign air of scorn, "that ten thousand piasters would not suffice?"

"Señor, I cannot give you a half real more!"

"Take away these caskets and bring me the sum I ask for. To complete the thirty thousand piasters which I need, you will take a mortgage on this house. Does it seem to you to be solid?"

"Ah, señor, in this city, subject to earthquakes, one knows not who lives or dies, who stands or falls."

And, as he said this, Samuel let himself fall on his heels several times to test the solidity of the floors.

"Well, to oblige your lordship, I will furnish you with the required sum; although, at this moment I ought not to part with money; for I am about to marry my daughter to the *caballero* André Certa. Do you know him, sir?"

"I do not know him, and I beg of you to send me this instant, the sum agreed upon. Take away these jewels."

"Will you have a receipt for them?" asked the Jew.

Don Vegal passed into the adjoining room, without replying.

"Proud Spaniard!" muttered Samuel, "I will crush thy insolence, as I disperse thy riches! By Solomon! I am a skillful man, since my interests keep pace with my sentiments."

Don Vegal, on leaving the Jew, had found Martin Paz in profound dejection of spirits, mingled with mortification.

"What is the matter?" he asked affectionately.

"Señor, it is the daughter of the Jew whom I love."

"A Jewess!" exclaimed Don Vegal, with disgust.

But seeing the sadness of the Indian, he added:

"Let us go, *amigo*, we will talk of these things afterward!"

An hour later, Martin Paz, clad in Spanish costume, left the city, accompanied by Don Vegal, who took none of his people with him.

The Baths of Chorillos are situated at two leagues from Lima. This Indian parish possesses a pretty church; during the hot season it is the rendezvous of the fashionable Limanian society. Public games, interdicted at Lima, are permitted at Chorillos during the whole summer. The señoras there display unwonted ardor, and, in decorating himself for these pretty partners, more than one rich cavalier has seen his fortune dissipated in a few nights.

Chorillos was still little frequented; so Don Vegal and Martin Paz retired to a pretty cottage, built on the sea-shore, could live in quiet contemplation of the vast plains of the Pacific Ocean.

The Marquis Don Vegal, belonging to one of the most ancient families of Peru, saw about to terminate in himself the noble line of which he was justly proud; so his countenance bore the impress of profound sadness. After having mingled for some time in political affairs, he had felt an inexpressible disgust for the incessant revolutions brought about to gratify personal ambition; he had withdrawn into a sort of solitude, interrupted only at rare intervals by the duties of strict politeness.

His immense fortune was daily diminishing. The neglect into which his vast domains had fallen for want of laborers, had compelled him to borrow at a disadvantage; but the prospect of approaching mediocrity did not alarm him; that carelessness natural to the Spanish race, joined to the ennui of a useless existence, had rendered him insensible to the menaces of the future. Formerly the husband of an adored wife, the father of a charming little girl, he had seen himself deprived, by a horrible event, of both these objects of his love. Since then, no bond of affection had attached him to earth, and he suffered his life to float at the will of events.

Don Vegal had thought his heart to be indeed dead, when he felt it palpitate at contact with that of Martin Paz. This ardent nature awoke fire beneath the ashes; the proud bearing of the Indian suited the chivalric hidalgo; and then, weary of the Spanish nobles, in whom he no longer had confidence, disgusted with the selfish mestizoes, who wished to aggrandize themselves at his expense, he took a pleasure in turning to that primitive race, who have disputed so valiantly the American soil with the soldiers of Pizarro.

According to the intelligence received by the marquis, the Indian passed for dead at Lima; but, looking on his attachment for the Jewess as worse than death itself, the Spaniard resolved doubly to save his guest, by leaving the daughter of Samuel to marry André Certa.

While Martin Paz felt an infinite sadness pervade his heart, Don Vegal avoided all allusion to the past, and conversed with the young Indian on indifferent subjects.

Meanwhile, one day, saddened by his gloomy preoccupations, the Spaniard said to him:

"Why, my friend, do you lower the nobility of your nature by a sentiment so much beneath you? Was not that bold Manco-Capac, whom his patriotism placed in the rank of heroes, your ancestor? There is a noble part left for a valiant man, who will not suffer himself to be overcome by an unworthy passion. Have you no heart to regain your independence?"

"We are laboring for this, señor," said the Indian; "and the day when my brethren shall rise *en masse* is perhaps not far distant."

"I understand you; you allude to the war for which your brethren are preparing among their mountains; at a signal they will descend on the city, arms in hand—and will be conquered as they have always been! See how your interests will disappear amid these perpetual revolutions of which Peru is the theatre, and which will ruin it entirely, Indians and Spaniards, to the profit of the mestizoes, who are neither."

"We will save it ourselves," exclaimed Martin Paz.

"Yes, you will save it if you understand how to play your part! Listen to me, Paz, you whom I love from day to day as a son! I say it with grief; but, we Spaniards, the degenerate sons of a powerful race, no longer have the energy necessary to elevate and govern a state. It is therefore yours to triumph over that unhappy Americanism, which tends to reject European colonization. Yes, know that only European emigration can save the old Peruvian empire. Instead of this intestine war which tends to exclude all castes, with the exception of one, frankly extend your hands to the industrious population of the Old World."

"The Indians, señor, will always see in strangers an enemy, and will never suffer them to breathe with impunity the air of their mountains. The kind of dominion which I exercise over them will be without effect on the day when I do not swear death to their oppressors, whoever they may be! And, besides, what am I now?" added Martin Paz, with great sadness; "a fugitive who would not have three hours to live in the streets of Lima."

"Paz, you must promise me that you will not return thither."

"How can I promise you this, Don Vegal? I speak only the truth, and I should perjure myself were I to take an oath to that effect."

Don Vegal was silent. The passion of the young Indian increased from day to day; the marquis trembled to see him incur certain death by re-appearing at Lima. He hastened by all his desires, he would have hastened by all his efforts, the marriage of the Jewess!

To ascertain himself the state of things he quitted Chorillos one morning, returned to the city, and learned that André Certa had recovered from his wound. His approaching marriage was the topic of general conversation.

Don Vegal wished to see this woman whose image troubled the mind of Martin Paz. He repaired, at evening, to the Plaza-Mayor. The crowd was always numerous there. There he met Father Joachim de Camarones, his confessor and his oldest friend; he acquainted him with his mode of life. What was the astonishment of the good father to learn the existence of Martin Paz. He promised Don Vegal to watch also himself over the young Indian, and to convey to the marquis any intelligence of importance.

Suddenly the glances of Don Vegal rested on a young girl, enveloped in a black mantle, reclining in a calêche.

"Who is that beautiful person?" asked he of the father.

"It is the betrothed of André Certa, the daughter of the Jew Samuel."

"She! the daughter of the Jew!"

The marquis could hardly suppress his astonishment, and, pressing the hand of Father Joachim, pensively took the road to Chorillos.

He had just recognized in Sarah, the pretended Jewess, the young girl whom he had seen praying with such Christian fervor, at the church of Santa Anna.

CHAPTER V.

THE HATRED OF THE INDIANS.

Since the Colombian troops, confided by Bolivar to the orders of General Santa Cruz, had been driven from lower Peru, this country, which had been incessantly agitated by *pronunciamentos*, military revolts, had recovered some calmness and tranquillity.

In fact, private ambition no longer had any thing to expect; the president Gambarra seemed immovable in his palace of the Plaza-Mayor. In this direction there was nothing to fear; but the true danger, concealed, imminent, was not from these rebellions, as promptly extinguished as kindled, and which seemed to flatter the taste of the Americans for military parades.

This unknown peril escaped the eyes of the Spaniards, too lofty to perceive it, and the attention of the mestizoes, who never wished to look beneath them.

And yet there was an unusual agitation among the Indians of the city; they often mingled with the *serranos*, the inhabitants of the mountains; these people seemed to have shaken off their natural apathy. Instead of rolling themselves in their *ponchos*, with their feet turned to the spring sun, they were scattered throughout the country, stopping one another, exchanging private signals, and haunting the least frequented *pulperias*, in which they could converse without danger.

This movement was principally to be observed on one of the squares remote from the centre of the city. At the corner of a street stood a house, of only one story, whose wretched appearance struck the eye disagreeably.

A tavern of the lowest order, a *chingana*, kept by an old Indian woman, offered to the lowest *zambos* the *chica*, beer of fermented maize, and the *quarapo*, a beverage made of the sugar-cane.

The concourse of Indians on this square took place only at certain hours, and principally when a long pole was raised on the roof of the inn as a signal of assemblage, then the *zambos* of every profession, the *capataz*, the *arrieros*, muleteers, the *carreteros*, carters, entered the *chingana*, one by one, and immediately disappeared in the great hall; the *padrona* (hostess) seemed very busy, and leaving to her servant the care of the shop, hastened to serve herself her usual customers.

A few days after the disappearance of Martin Paz, there was a numerous assembly in the hall of the inn; one could scarcely through the darkness, rendered still more obscure by the tobacco-smoke, distinguish the frequenters of this tavern. Fifty Indians were ranged around a long table; some were chewing the *coca*, a kind of tea-leaf, mingled with a little piece of fragrant earth called *manubi*; others were drinking from large pots of fermented maize; but these occupations did not distract their attention, and they were closely listening to the speech of an Indian.

This was the Sambo, whose fixed eyes were strangely wild. He was clad as on the Plaza-Mayor.

After having carefully observed his auditors, the Sambo commenced in these terms:

"The children of the Sun can converse on grave affairs; there is no perfidious ear to hear them; on the square, some of our friends, disguised as street-singers, will attract the attention of the passers-by, and we shall enjoy entire liberty."

In fact the tones of a mandoline and of a *viguela* were echoingwithout.

The Indians within, knowing themselves in safety, lent therefore close attention to the words of the Sambo, in whom they placed entire confidence.

"What news can the Sambo give us of Martin Paz?" asked an Indian.

"None—is he dead or not? The Great Spirit only knows. I am expecting some of our brethren, who have descended the river to its mouth, perhaps they will have found the body of Martin Paz."

"He was a good chief," said Manangani, a ferocious Indian, much dreaded; "but why was he not at his post on the day when the schooner brought us arms?"

The Sambo cast down his head without reply.

"Did not my brethren know," resumed Manangani, "that there was an exchange of shots between the *Annonciation* and the custom-house officers, and that the capture of the vessel would have ruined our projects of conspiracy?"

A murmur of approbation received the words of the Indian.

"Those of my brethren who will wait before they judge will be the beloved of my heart," resumed the Sambo; "who knows whether my son Martin Paz will not one day re-appear? Listen now; the arms which have been sent us from Sechura are in our power; they are concealed in the mountains of the Cordilleras, and ready to do their office when you shall be prepared to do your duty."

"And what delays us?" said a young Indian; "we have sharpened our knives and are waiting."

"Let the hour come," said the Sambo; "do my brethren know what enemy their arms should strike first?"

"Those mestizoes who treat us as slaves, and strike us with the hand and whip, like restive mules."

"These are the monopolizers of the riches of the soil, who will not suffer us to purchase a little comfort for our old age."

"You are mistaken; and your first blows must be struck elsewhere," said the Sambo, growing animated; "these are not the men who have dared for three hundred years past to tread the soil of our ancestors; it is not these rich men gorged with gold who have dragged to the tomb the sons of Manco-Capac; no, it is these proud Spaniards whom Fate has thrust on our independent shores! These are the true conquerors of whom you are the true slaves! If they have no longer wealth, they have authority; and, in spite of Peruvian emancipation, they crush and trample upon our natural rights. Let us forget what we are, to remember what our fathers have been!"

"*Anda! anda!*" exclaimed the assembly, with stamps of approbation.

After a few moments of silence, the Sambo assured himself, by interrogating various conspirators, that the friends of Cusco and of all Bolivia were ready to strike as a single man.

Then, resuming with fire:

"And our brethren of the mountains, brave Manangani, if they have all a heart of hatred equal to thine, a courage equal to thine, they will fall on Lima like an avalanche from the summit of the Cordilleras."

"The Sambo shall not complain of their boldness on the day appointed. Let the Indian leave the city, he shall not go far without seeing throng around him *zambos* burning for vengeance! In the gorges of San Cristoval and the Amancaës, more than one is couched on his *poncho*, with his poignard at his girdle, waiting until a long carbine shall be confided to his skillful hand. They also have not forgotten that they have to revenge on the vain Spaniards the defeat of Manco-Capac."

"Well said! Manangani; it is the god of hatred who speaks from thy mouth. My brethren shall know before long him whom their chiefs have chosen to lead this great vengeance. President Gambarra is seeking only to consolidate his power; Bolivar is afar, Santa Cruz has been driven away; we can act with certainty. In a few days, the fête of the Amancaës will summon our oppressors to pleasure; then, let each be ready to march, and let the news be carried to the most remote villages of Bolivia."

At this moment three Indians entered the great hall. The Sambo hastened to meet them.

"Well?" said he to them.

"The body of Martin Paz has not been recovered; we have sounded the river in every direction; our most skillful divers have explored it with religious care, and the son of the Sambo cannot have perished in the waters of the Rimac."

"Have they killed him? What has become of him? Oh! wo, wo to them if they have killed my son! Let my brethren separate in silence; let each return to his post, look, watch and wait!"

The Indians went out and dispersed; the Sambo alone remained with Manangani, who asked him:

"Does the Sambo know what sentiment conducted his son to San Lazaro? The Sambo, I trust, is sure of his son?"

The eyes of the Indian flashed, and the blood mounted to his cheek. The ferocious Manangani recoiled.

But the Indian controlled himself, and said:

"If Martin Paz has betrayed his brethren, I will first kill all those to whom he has given his friendship, all those to whom he has given his love! Then I will kill him, and myself afterward, that nothing may be left beneath the sun of an infamous, and dishonored race."

At this moment, the *padrona* opened the door of the room, advanced toward the Sambo, and handed him a billet directed to his address.

"Who gave you this?" said he.

"I do not know; this paper may have been designedly forgotten by a *chica*-drinker. I found it on the table."

"Have there been any but Indians here?"

"There have been none but Indians."

The *padrona* went out; the Sambo unfolded the billet, and read aloud:

"A young girl has prayed for the return of Martin Paz, for she has not forgotten that the young Indian protected her and risked his life for her. If the Sambo has any news of his poor son, or any hope of finding him, let him surround his arm with a red handkerchief; there are eyes which see him pass daily."

The Sambo crushed the billet in his hand.

"The unhappy boy," said he, "has suffered himself to be caught by the eyes of a woman."

"Who is this woman?" asked Manangani.

"It is not an Indian," replied the Sambo, observing the billet; "it is some young girl of the other classes. Martin Paz, I no longer know thee!"

"Shall you do what this woman requests?"

"No," replied the Indian, violently; "let her lose all hope of seeing him again; let her die, if she will."

And the Sambo tore the billet in a rage.

"It must have been an Indian who brought this billet," observed Manangani.

"Oh, it cannot have been one of ours! He must have known that I often came to this inn, but I will set my foot in it no more We have occupied ourselves long enough with trifling affairs," resumed he, coldly; "let my brother return to the mountains; I will remain to watch over the city. We shall see whether the fête of the Amancaës will be joyous for the oppressors or the oppressed!"

The two Indians separated.

The plan of the conspiracy was well conceived and the hour of its execution well chosen. Peru, almost depopulated, counted only a small number of Spaniards and mestizoes. The invasion of the Indians, gathered from every direction, from the forests of Brazil, as well as the mountains of Chili and the plains of La Plata, would cover the theatre of war with a formidable army. The great cities, like Lima, Cusco, Puña, might be utterly destroyed; and it was not to be expected that the Colombian troops, so recently driven away by the Peruvian government, would come to the assistance of their enemies in peril.

This social overturn might therefore have succeeded, if the secret had remained buried in the hearts of the Indians, and there surely could not be traitors among them?

But they were ignorant that a man had obtained private audience of the President Gambarra. This man informed him that the schooner *Annonciation* had been captured from him by Indian pirates That it had been laden with arms of all sorts; that canoes had unloaded it at the mouth of the Rimac; and he claimed a high indemnity for the service he thus rendered to the Peruvian government.

And yet this man had let his vessel to the agents of the Sambo; he had received for it a considerable sum, and had come to sell the secret which he had surprised.

By these traits the reader will recognize the Jew Samuel.

CHAPTER VI.

THE BETROTHAL.

André Certa, entirely recovered, sure of the death of Martin Paz, pressed his marriage: he was impatient to parade the young and beautiful Jewess through the streets of Lima.

Sarah constantly manifested toward him a haughty indifference; but he cared not for it, considering her as an article of sale, for which he had paid a hundred thousand piasters.

And yet André Certa suspected the Jew, and with good reason; if the contract was dishonorable, the contractors were still more so. So the mestizo wished to have a secret interview with Samuel, and took him one day to the Baths of Chorillos.

He was not sorry, besides, to try the chances of play before his wedding: public gaming, prohibited at Lima, is perfectly tolerated elsewhere. The passion of the Limanian ladies and gentlemen for this hazardous amusement is singular and irresistible.

The games were open some days before the arrival of the Marquis Don Vegal; thenceforth there was a perpetual movement of the populace on the road from Lima: some came on foot, who returned in carriages; others were about to risk and lose the last remnants of their fortunes.

Don Vegal and Martin Paz took no part in these exciting pleasures. The reveries of the young Indian had more noble causes; he was thinking of Sarah and of his benefactor.

The concourse of the Limanians to the Baths of Chorillos was without danger for him; little known by the inhabitants of the city, like all the mountain Indians he easily concealed himself from all eyes.

After his evening walk with the marquis, Martin Paz would return to his room, and leaning his elbow on the window, pass long hours in allowing his tumultuous thoughts to wander over the Pacific Ocean. Don Vegal lodged in a neighboring chamber, and guarded him with paternal tenderness.

The Spaniard always remembered the daughter of Samuel, whom he had so unexpectedly seen at prayer in the Catholic temple. But he had not dared to confide this important secret to Martin Paz while instructing him by degrees in Christian truths; he feared to re-animate sentiments which he wished to extinguish—for the poor Indian, unknown and proscribed, must renounce all hope of happiness! Father Joachim kept Don Vegal informed of the progress of affairs: the police had at last ceased to trouble themselves about Martin Paz; and with time and the influence of his protector, the Indian, become a man of merit and capable of great things, might one day take rank in the highest Peruvian society.

Weary of the uncertainty into which his incognito plunged him, Paz resolved to know what had become of the young Jewess. Thanks to his Spanish costume, he could glide into a gaming-saloon, and listen to the conversation of its various frequenters. André Certa was a man of so much importance, that his marriage, if it was approaching, would be the subject of conversation.

One evening, instead of directing his steps toward the sea, the Indian climbed over the high rocks on which the principal habitations of Chorillos are built; a house, fronted by broad stone steps, struck his eyes—he entered it without noise.

The day had been hard for many of the wealthy Limanians; some among them, exhausted with the fatigues of the preceding night, were reposing on the ground, wrapped in their *ponchos*.

Other players were seated before a large green table, divided into four compartments by two lines, which intersected each other at the centre in right angles; on each of these compartments were the first letters of the words *azar* and *suerte*, (chance and fate,) A and S.

At this moment, the parties of the *monte* were animated; a mestizo was pursuing the unfavorable chance with feverish ardor.

"Two thousand piasters!" exclaimed he.

The banker shook the dice, and the player burst into imprecations.

"Four thousand piasters!" said he, again. And he lost once more.

Martin Paz, protected by the obscurity of the saloon, could look the player in the face, and he turned pale.

It was André Certa!

Near him, was standing the Jew Samuel.

"You have played enough, Señor André," said Samuel to him; "the luck is not for you."

"What business is it of yours?" replied the mestizo, roughly.

Samuel bent down to his ear.

"If it is not my business, it is your business to break off these habits during the days which precede your marriage."

"Eight thousand piasters!" resumed André Certa.

He lost again: the mestizo suppressed a curse and the banker resumed—"Play on!"

André Certa, drawing from his pocket some bills, was about to have hazarded a considerable sum; he had even deposited it on one of the tables, and the banker, shaking his dice, was about to have decided its fate, when a sign from Samuel stopped him short. The Jew bent again to the ear of the mestizo, and said—

"If nothing remains to you to conclude our bargain, it shall be broken off this evening!"

André Certa shrugged his shoulders, took up his money, and went out.

"Continue now," said Samuel to the banker; "you may ruin this gentleman after his marriage."

The banker bowed submissively. The Jew Samuel was the founder and proprietor of the games of Chorillos. Wherever there was a *real* to be made this man was to be met with.

He followed the mestizo; and finding him on the stone steps, said to him—

"I have secrets of importance to communicate. Where can we converse in safety?"

"Wherever you please," replied Certa, roughly.

"Señor, let not your passions ruin your prospects. I would neither confide my secret to the most carefully closed chambers, nor the most lonely plains. If you pay me dearly for it, it is because it is worth telling and worth keeping."

As they spoke thus, these two men had reached the sea, near the cabins destined for the use of the bathers. They knew not that they were seen, heard and watched by Martin Paz, who glided like a serpent in the shadow.

"Let us take a canoe," said André, "and go out into the open sea; the sharks may, perhaps, show themselves discreet."

André detached from the shore a little boat, and threw some money to its guardian. Samuel embarked with him, and the mestizo pushed off. He vigorously plied two flexible oars, which soon took them a mile from the shore.

But as he saw the canoe put off, Martin Paz, concealed in a crevice of the rock, hastily undressed, and precipitating himself into the sea, swam vigorously toward the boat.

The sun had just buried his last rays in the waves of the ocean, and darkness hovered over the crests of the waves.

Martin Paz had not once reflected that sharks of the most dangerous species frequented these fatal shores. He stopped not far from the boat of the mestizo, and listened.

"But what proof of the identity of the daughter shall I carry to the father?" asked André Certa of the Jew.

"You will recall to him the circumstances under which he lost her."

"What were these circumstances?"

Martin Paz, now scarcely above the waves, listened without understanding. In a girdle attached to his body, he had a poignard; he waited.

"Her father," said the Jew, "lived at Concencion, in Chili: he was then the great nobleman he is now; only his fortune equalled his nobility. Obliged to come to Lima on business, he set out alone, leaving at Concencion his wife, and child aged fifteen months. The climate of Peru agreed with him, and he sent for the marchioness to rejoin him. She embarked on the *San-José* of Valparaiso, with her confidential servants.

"I was going to Peru in the same ship. The *San-José* was about to enter the harbor of Lima; but, near Juan Fernandez, was struck by a terrific hurricane, which disabled her and threw her on her side—it was the affair of half an hour. The *San-José* filled with water and was slowly sinking; the passengers and crew took refuge in the boat, but at sight of the furious waves, the marchioness refused to enter it; she pressed her infant in her arms, and remained in the ship. I remained with her—the boat was swallowed up at a hundred fathoms from the *San-José*, with all her crew. We were alone—the tempest blew with increasing violence. As my fortune was not on board, I had nothing to lose. The *San-José*, having five feet of water in her hold, drifted on the rocks of the shore, where she broke to pieces. The young woman was thrown into the sea with her daughter: fortunately, for me," said the Jew, with a gloomy smile, "I could seize the child, and reach the shore with it."

"All these details are exact?"

"Perfectly so. The father will recognize them. I had done a good day's work, señor; since she is worth to me the hundred thousand piasters which you are about to pay me. Now, let the marriage take place to-morrow."

"What does this mean?" asked Martin Paz of himself, still swimming in the shadow.

"Here is my pocket-book, with the hundred thousand piasters—take it, Master Samuel," replied André Certa to the Jew.

"Thanks, Señor André," said the Israelite, seizing the treasure; "take this receipt in exchange—I pledge myself to restore you double this sum, if you do not become a member of one of the proudest families of Spain."

But the Indian had not heard this last sentence; he had dived to avoid the approach of the boat, and his eyes could see a shapeless mass gliding rapidly toward him. He thought it was the canoe—he was mistaken.

It was a *tintorea*; a shark of the most ferocious species.

Martin Paz did not quail, or he would have been lost. The animal approached him—the Indian dived; but he was obliged to come up, in order to breathe.... He looked at the sky, as if he was never to behold it again. The stars sparkled above his head; the *tintorea* continued to approach. A vigorous blow with his tail struck the swimmer; Martin Paz felt his slimy scales brush his breast. The shark, in order to snatch at him, turned on his back and opened his jaws, armed with a triple row of teeth. Martin Paz saw the white belly of the animal gleam beneath the wave, and with a rapid hand struck it with his poignard.

Suddenly he found the waters around him red with blood. He dived—came up again at ten fathoms' distance—thought of the daughter of Samuel; and seeing nothing more of the boat of the mestizo, regained the shore in a few strokes, already forgetting that he had just escaped death.

He quickly rejoined Don Vegal. The latter, not having found him on his return, was anxiously awaiting him. Paz made no allusion to his recent adventures; but seemed to take a lively pleasure in his conversation.

But the next day Martin Paz had left Chorillos, and Don Vegal, tortured with anxiety, hastily returned to Lima.

The marriage of André Certa with the daughter of the wealthy Samuel, was an important event. The beautiful señoras had not given themselves a moment's rest; they had exhausted their ingenuity to invent some pretty corsage or novel head-dress; they had wearied themselves in trying without cessation the most varied toilets.

Numerous preparations were also going on in the house of Samuel; it was a part of the Jew's plan to give great publicity to the marriage of Sarah. The frescoes which adorned his dwelling according to the Spanish custom, had been newly painted; the richest hangings fell in large folds at the windows and doors of the habitation. Furniture carved in the latest fashion, of precious or fragrant wood, was crowded in vast saloons, impregnated with a delicious coolness. Rare shrubs, the productions of warm countries, seized the eye with their splendid colors, and one would have thought Spring had stolen along the balconies and terraces, to inundate them with flowers and perfumes.

Meanwhile, amid these smiling marvels, the young girl was weeping; Sarah no longer had hope, since the Sambo had none; and the Sambo had no hope, since he wore no sign of hope! The negro Liberta had watched the steps of the old Indian; he had seen nothing. Ah! if the poor child could have followed the impulses of her heart, she would have immured herself in one of those tranquil *beaterios*, to die there amid tears and prayer.

Urged by an irresistible attraction to the doctrines of Catholicism, the young Jewess had been secretly converted; by the cares of the good Father Joachim, she had been won over to a religion more in accordance with her feelings than that in which she had been educated. If Samuel had destined her for a Jew, she would have avowed her faith; but, about to espouse a Catholic, she reserved for her husband the secret of her conversion.

Father Joachim, in order to avoid scandal, and besides, better read in his breviary than in the human heart, had suffered Sarah to believe in the death of Martin Paz. The conversion of the young girl was the most important thing to him; he saw it assured by her union with André Certa, and he sought to accustom her to the idea of this marriage, the conditions of which he was far from respecting.

At last the day so joyous for some, so sad for others, had arrived. André Certa had invited the entire city to his nuptials; his invitations were refused by the noble families, who excused themselves on various pretexts. The mestizo, meanwhile, proudly held up his head, and scarcely looked at those of his own class. The little Milleflores in vain essayed his humblest vows; but he consoled himself with the idea that he was about to figure as an active party in the repast which was to follow.

In the meantime, the young mestizoes were discoursing with him in the brilliant saloons of the Jew, and the crowd of guests thronged around André Certa, who proudly displayed the splendors of his toilet.

The contract was soon to be signed; the sun had long been set, and the young girl had not appeared.

Doubtless she was discussing with her duenna and her maids the place of a ribbon or the choice of an ornament. Perhaps, that enchanting timidity which so beautifully adorns the cheeks of a young girl, detained her still from their inquisitive regards.

The Jew Samuel seemed a prey to secret uneasiness; André Certa bent his brow in an impatient manner; a sort of embarrassment was depicted on the countenance of more than one guest, while the thousand of wax-lights, reflected by the mirrors, filled the saloon with dazzling splendor.

Without, a man was wandering in mortal anxiety; it was the Marquis Don Vegal.

CHAPTER VII.

ALL INTERESTS AT STAKE.

Meanwhile, Sarah was left alone, alone with her anguish and her grief! She was about to give up her whole life to a man whom she did not love! She leaned over the perfumed balcony of her chamber, which overlooked the interior gardens. Through the green jalousies, her ear listened to the sounds of the slumbering country. Her lace mantle, gliding over her arms, revealed a profusion of diamonds sparkling on her shoulders. Her sorrow, proud and majestic, appeared through all her ornaments, and she might have been taken for one of those beautiful Greek slaves, nobly draped in their antique garments.

Suddenly her glance rested on a man who was gliding silently among the avenues of the magnolia; she recognized him; it was Liberta, her servant. He seemed to be watching some invisible enemy, now sheltering himself behind a statue, now crouching on the ground.

Sarah was afraid, and looked around her. She was alone, entirely alone. Her eyes rested on the gardens, and she became pale, paler still! Before her was transpiring a terrible scene. Liberta was in the grasp of a man of tall stature, who had thrown him down; stifled sighs proved that a robust hand was pressing the lips of the Indian.

The young girl, summoning all her courage, was about to cry out, when she saw the two men rise! The negro was looking fixedly at his adversary.

"It is you, then! it is you!" exclaimed he.

And he followed this man in a strange stupefaction. They arrived beneath the balcony of Sarah. Suddenly, before she had time to utter a cry, Martin Paz appeared to her, like a phantom from another world; and, like the negro when overthrown by the Indian, the young girl, bending before the glance of Martin Paz, could in her turn only repeat these words,

"It is you, then! it is you!"

The young Indian fixed on her his motionless eyes, and said:

"Does the betrothed hear the sound of the festival? The guests are thronging into the saloons to see happiness radiate from her countenance! Is it then a victim, prepared for the sacrifice, who is about to present herself to their impatient eyes? Is it with these features, pale with sorrow, with eyes in which sparkle bitter tears, that the young girl is to appear herself before her betrothed?"

Martin Paz spoke thus, in a tone full of sympathizing sadness, and Sarah listened vaguely as to those harmonies which we hear in dreams!

The young Indian resumed with infinite sweetness:

"Since the soul of the young girl is in mourning, let her look beyond the house of her father, beyond the city where she suffers and weeps; beyond the mountains, the palm-trees lift up their heads in freedom, the birds strike the air with an independent wing; men have immensity to live in, and the young girls may unfold their spirits and their hearts!"

Sarah raised her head toward Martin Paz. The Indian had drawn himself up to his full height, and with his arm extended toward the summits of the Cordilleras, was pointing out to the young girl the path to liberty.

Sarah felt herself constrained by an irresistible force. Already the sound of voices reached her; they approached her chamber; her father was undoubtedly about to enter; perhaps her lover would accompany him! The Indian suddenly extinguished the lamp suspended above his head. A whistling, similar to the cry of the *cilguero*, and reminding one of that heard on the Plaza-Mayor, pierced the silent darkness of night; the young girl swooned.

The door opened hastily; Samuel and André Certa entered. The darkness was profound; some servants ran with torches. The chamber was empty.

"Death and fury!" exclaimed the mestizo.

"Where is she?" asked Samuel.

"You are responsible for her," said André, brutally.

At these words, the Jew felt a cold sweat freeze even his bones.

"Help! help!" he exclaimed.

And, followed by his domestics, he sprang out of the house.

Martin Paz fled rapidly through the streets of the city. The negro Liberta followed him; but did not appear disposed to dispute with him the possession of the young girl.

At two hundred paces from the dwelling of the Jew, Paz found some Indians of his companions, who had assembled at the whistle uttered by him.

"To our mountain *ranchos*!" exclaimed he.

"To the house of the Marquis Don Vegal!" said another voice behind him.

Martin Paz turned; the Spaniard was at his side.

"Will you not confide this young girl to me?" asked the marquis.

The Indian bent his head, and said in a low voice to his companions:

"To the dwelling of the Marquis Don Vegal!"

They turned their steps in this direction.

An extreme confusion reigned then in the saloons of the Jew. The news of Sarah's disappearance was a thunderbolt; the friends of André hastened to follow him. The *faubourg* of San Lazaro was explored, hastily searched; but nothing could be discovered. Samuel tore his hair in despair. During the whole night the most active research was useless.

"Martin Paz is living!" exclaimed André Certa, in a moment of fury.

And the presentiment quickly acquired confirmation. The police were immediately informed of the elopement; its most active agents bestirred themselves; the Indians were closely watched, and if the retreat of the young girl was not discovered, evident proofs of an approaching revolt came to light, which accorded with the denunciations of the Jew.

André Certa lavished gold freely, but could learn nothing. Meanwhile, the gate-keepers declared that they had seen no person leave Lima; the young girl must therefore be concealed in the city.

Liberta, who returned to his master, was often interrogated; but no person seemed more astonished than himself at the elopement of Sarah.

Meanwhile, one man besides André Certa had seen in the disappearance of the young Jewess, a proof of the existence of Martin Paz; it was the Sambo. He was wandering in the streets of Lima, when the cry uttered by the Indian fixed his attention; it was a signal of rally well known to him! The Sambo was therefore a spectator of the capture of the young girl, and followed her to the dwelling of the marquis.

The Spaniard entered by a secret door, of which he alone had the key; so that his domestics suspected nothing. Martin Paz carried the young girl in his arms and laid her on a bed.

When Don Vegal, who had returned to re-enter by the principal door, reached the chamber where Sarah was reposing, he found Martin Paz kneeling beside her. The marquis was about to reproach the Indian with his conduct, when the latter said to him:

"You see, my father, whether I love you! Ah! why did you throw yourself in my way? We should have been already free in our mountains. But how, should I not have obeyed your words?"

Don Vegal knew not what to reply, his heart was seized with a powerful emotion. He felt how much he was beloved by Martin Paz.

"The day on which Sarah shall quit your dwelling to be restored to her father and her betrothed," sighed the Indian, "you will have a son and a friend less in the world."

As he said these last words, Paz moistened with his tears the hand of Don Vegal. They were the first tears this man had shed!

The reproaches of Don Vegal died away before this respectful submission. The young girl had become his guest; she was sacred! He could not help admiring Sarah, still in a swoon; he was prepared to love her, of whose conversion he had been a witness, and whom he would have been pleased to bestow as a companion upon the young Indian.

It was then that, on opening her eyes, Sarah found herself in the presence of a stranger.

"Where am I?" said she, with a sentiment of terror.

"With a generous man who has permitted me to call him my father," replied Martin Paz, pointing to the Spaniard.

The young girl, restored by the voice of the Indian to a consciousness of her position, covered her face with her trembling hands, and began to sob.

"Withdraw, friend," said Don Vegal to the young man; "withdraw."

Martin Paz slowly left the room, not without having pressed the hand of the Spaniard, and cast on Sarah a lingering look.

Then Don Vegal bestowed upon this poor child consolations of exquisite delicacy; he conveyed in suitable language his sentiments of nobility and honor. Attentive and resigned, the young girl comprehended what danger she had escaped; and she confided her future happiness to the care of the Spaniard. But amid phrases interrupted by sighs and mingled with tears, Don Vegal perceived the intense attachment of this simple heart for him whom she called her deliverer. He induced Sarah to take some repose, and watched over her with the solicitude of a father.

Martin Paz comprehended the duties that honor required of him, and, in spite of perils and dangers, would not pass the night beneath the roof of Don Vegal.

He therefore went out; his head was burning, his blood was boiling with fever in his veins.

He had not gone a hundred paces in the street, when five or six men threw themselves upon him, and, notwithstanding his obstinate defense, succeeded in binding him. Martin Paz uttered a cry of despair, which was lost in the night. He believed himself in the power of his enemies, and gave a last thought to the young girl.

A short time afterward the Indian was deposited in a room. The bandage which had covered his eyes was taken off. He looked around him, and saw himself in the lower hall of that tavern where his brethren had organized their approaching revolt.

The Sambo, Manangani, and others, surrounded him. A gleam of indignation flashed from his eyes, which was reciprocated by his captors.

"My son had then no pity on my tears," said the Sambo, "since he suffered me for so long a time to believe in his death?"

"Is it on the eve before a revolt that Martin Paz, our chief, should be found in the camp of our enemies?"

Martin Paz replied neither to his father, nor to Manangani.

"So our most important interests have been sacrificed to a woman!"

As he spoke thus, Manangani had approached Martin Paz; a poignard was gleaming in his hand. Martin Paz did not even look at him.

"Let us first speak," said the Sambo; "we will act afterward. If my son fails to conduct his brethren to the combat, I shall know now on whom to avenge his treason. Let him take care! the daughter of the Jew Samuel is not so well concealed that she can escape our hatred. My son will reflect. Struck with a mortal condemnation, proscribed, wandering among our masters, he will not have a stone on which to rest his sorrows. If, on the contrary, we resume our ancient country and our ancient power, Martin Paz, the chief of numerous tribes, may bestow upon his betrothed both happiness and glory."

Martin Paz remained silent; but a terrific conflict was going on within him. The Sambo had roused the most sensitive chords of his proud nature to vibrate; placed between a life of fatigues, of dangers, of despair, and an existence happy, honored, illustrious, he could not hesitate. But should he then abandon the Marquis Don Vegal, whose noble hopes destined him as the deliverer of Peru!

"Oh!" thought he, as he looked at his father, "they will kill Sarah, if I forsake them."

"What does my son reply to us?" imperiously demanded the Sambo.

"That Martin Paz is indispensable to your projects; that he enjoys a supreme authority over the Indians of the city; that he leads them at his will, and, at a sign, could have them dragged to death. He must therefore resume his place in the revolt, in order to ensure victory."

The bonds which still enchained him were detached by order of the Sambo; Martin Paz arose free among his brethren.

"My son," said the Indian, who was observing him attentively, "to-morrow, during the fête of the Amancaës, our brethren will fall like an avalanche on the unarmed Limanians. There is the road to the Cordilleras, there is the road to the city; you will go wherever your good pleasure shall lead you. To- morrow! to-morrow! you will find more than one mestizo breast to break your poignard against. You are free."

"To the mountains!" exclaimed Martin Paz, with a stern voice.

The Indian had again become an Indian amid the hatred which surrounded him.

"To the mountains," repeated he, "and wo to our enemies, wo!"

And the rising sun illumined with its earliest rays the council of the Indian chiefs in the heart of the Cordilleras.

These rays were joyless to the heart of the poor young girl, who wept and prayed. The marquis had summoned Father Joachim; and the worthy man had there met his beloved penitent. What happiness was it for her to kneel at the feet of the old priest, and to pour out her anguish and her afflictions.

But Sarah could not longer remain in the dwelling of the Spaniard. Father Joachim suggested this to Don Vegal, who knew not what part to take, for he was a prey to extreme anxiety. What had become of Martin Paz? He had fled the house. Was he in the power of his enemies? Oh! how the Spaniard regretted having suffered him to leave it during that night of alarms! He sought him with the ardor, with the affection of a father; he found him not.

"My old friend," said he to Joachim, "the young girl is in safety near you; do not leave her during this fatal night."

"But her father, who seeks her—her betrothed, who awaits her?"

"One day—one single day! You know not whose existence is bound to that of this child. One day—one single day! at least until I find Martin Paz, he whom my heart and God have named my son!"

Father Joachim returned to the young girl; Don Vegal went out and traversed the streets of Lima.

The Spaniard was surprised at the noise, the commotion, the agitation of the city. It was that the great fête of the Amancaës, forgotten by him alone, the

24th of June, the day of St. John, had arrived. The neighboring mountains were covered with verdure and flowers; the inhabitants, on foot, on horseback, in carriages, were repairing to a celebrated table-land, situated at half a league from Lima, where the spectators enjoyed an admirable prospect; mestizoes and Indians mingled in the common fête; they walked gayly by groups of relatives or friends; each group, calling itself by the name of *partida*, carried its provisions, and was preceded by a player on the guitar, who chanted, accompanying himself, the most popular *yaravis* and *llantos*. These joyous promenaders advanced with cries, sports, endless jests, through the fields of maize and of *alfalfa*, through the groves of banana, whose fruits hung to the ground; they traversed those beautiful *alamedas*, planted with willows, and forests of citron, and orange-trees, whose intoxicating perfumes were mingled with the wild fragrance from the mountains. All along the road, traveling cabarets offered to the promenaders the brandy of *pisco* and the *chica*, whose copious libations excited to laughter and clamor; cavaliers made their horses caracole in the midst of the throng, and rivaled each other in swiftness, address, and dexterity; all the dances in vogue, from the *loudon* to the *mismis*, from the *boleros* to the *zamacuecas*, agitated and hurried on the *caballeros* and black-eyed *sambas*. The sounds of the *viguela* were soon no longer sufficient for the disordered movements of the dancers; the musicians uttered wild cries, which stimulated them to delirium; the spectators beat the measure with their feet and hands, and the exhausted couples sunk one after another to the ground.

There reigned in this fête, which derives its name from the little mountain-flowers, an inconceivable transport and freedom; and yet no private brawl mingled among the cries of public rejoicing; a few lancers on horseback, ornamented with their shining cuirasses, maintained here and there order among the populace.

The various classes of Limanian society mingled in these rejoicings, which are repeated every day throughout the month of July. Pretty *tapadas* laughingly elbow beautiful girls, who bravely come, with uncovered faces, to meet joyous cavaliers; and when at last this multitude arrive at the *plateau* of the Amancaës, an immense clamor of admiration is repeated by the mountain echoes.

At the feet of the spectators extends the ancient city of kings, proudly lifting toward heaven its towers and its steeples, whose bells are ringing joyous peals. San Pedro, Saint Augustine, the Cathedral, attract the eye to their roofs, resplendent with the rays of the sun. San Domingo, the rich church, the Madonna of which is never clad in the same garments two days in succession, raises above her neighbors her tapering spire; on the right, the vast plains of the Pacific Ocean are undulating to the breath of the occidental breeze, and the eye, as it roves from Callao to Lima, rests on those funereal *chulpas*, the last remains of the great dynasty of the Incas; at the horizon, Cape Morro- Solar frames, with its sloping hills, the wonderful splendors of this picture.

So the Limanians are never satisfied with these admirable prospects, and their noisy approbation deafens every year the echoes of San Cristoval and the Amancaës.

Now, while they fearlessly enjoyed these picturesque views, and were giving themselves up to an irresistible delight, a gloomy bloody funereal drama was preparing on the snowy summits of the Cordilleras.

CHAPTER VIII.

CONQUERORS AND CONQUERED.

A prey to his blind grief, Don Vegal walked at random. After having lost his daughter, the hope of his race and of his love, was he about to see himself also deprived of the child of his adoption whom he had wrested from death? Don Vegal had forgotten Sarah, to think only of Martin Paz.

He was struck with the great number of Indians, of *zambos*, of *chiños*, who were wandering about the streets; these men, who usually took an active part in the sports of the Amancaës, were now walking silently with singular pre-occupation. Often some busy chief gave them a secret order, and went on his way; and all, notwithstanding their *detours*, were assembling by degrees in the wealthiest quarters of Lima, in proportion as the Limanians were scattered abroad in the country.

Don Vegal, absorbed in his own researches, soon forgot this singular state of things. He traversed San Lazaro throughout, saw André Certa there, enraged and armed, and the Jew Samuel, in the extremity of distress, not for the loss of his daughter, but for the loss of his hundred thousand piasters; but he found not Martin Paz, whom he was impatiently seeking. He ran to the consistorial prison. Nothing! He returned home. Nothing! He mounted his horse and hastened to Chorillos. Nothing! He returned at last, exhausted with fatigue, to Lima; the clock of the cathedral was striking four.

Don Vegal remarked some groups of Indians before his dwelling; but he could not, without compromising the man of whom he was in search, ask them—

"Where is Martin Paz?"

He re-entered, more despairing than ever.

Immediately a man emerged from a neighboring alley, and came directly to the Indians. This man was the Sambo.

"The Spaniard has returned," said he to them; "you know him now; he is one of the representatives of the race which crushes us—wo to him!"

"And when shall we strike?"

"When five o'clock sounds, and the tocsin from the mountain gives the signal of vengeance."

Then the Sambo marched with hasty steps to the *chingana*, and rejoined the chief of the revolt.

Meanwhile the sun had begun to sink beneath the horizon; it was the hour in which the Limanian aristocracy went in its turn to the Amancaës; the richest toilets shone in the equipages which defiled to the right and left beneath the trees along the road; there was an inextricable mêlée of foot-passengers, carriages, horses; a confusion of cries, songs, instruments, and vociferations.

The clock on the tower of the cathedral suddenly struck five! and a shrill funereal sound vibrated through the air; the tocsin thundered over the crowd, frozen in its delirium.

An immense cry resounded in the city. From every square, every street, every house issued the Indians, with arms in their hands, and fury in their eyes. The principal places of the city were thronged with these men, some of whom shook above their heads burning torches!

"Death to the Spaniards! death to the oppressors!" such was the watch-word of the rebels.

Those who attempted to return to Lima must have recoiled before these masses; but the summits of the hills were quickly covered with other enemies, and all retreat was impossible; the *zambos* precipitated themselves like a thunderbolt on this crowd, exhausted with the fatigues of the festival, while the mountain Indians cleared for themselves a bloody path to rejoin their brethren of the city.

Imagine the aspect presented by Lima at this terrible moment. The rebels had left the square of the tavern, and were scattered in all quarters; at the head of one of the columns, Martin Paz was waving the black flag—the flag of independence; while the Indians in the other streets were attacking the houses appointed to ruin, Martin Paz took possession of the Plaza-Mayor with his company; near him, Manangani was uttering ferocious yells, and proudly displaying his bloody arms.

But the soldiers of the government, forewarned of the revolt, were ranged in battle array before the palace of the president; a frightful *fusillade* greeted the insurgents at their entrance on the square; surprised by this unexpected discharge, which extended a goodly number of them on the ground, they sprang upon the troops with insurmountable impatience; a horrible mêlée followed, in which men fought body to body. Martin Paz and Manangani performed prodigies of valor, and escaped death only by miracle.

It was necessary at all hazards that the palace should be taken and occupied by their men.

"Forward!" cried Martin Paz, and his voice led the Indians to the assault.

Although they were crushed in every direction, they succeeded in making the body of troops around the palace recoil. Already had Manangani sprang on the first steps; but he suddenly stopped as the opening ranks of soldiers unmasked two pieces of cannon ready to fire on the assailants.

There was not a moment to lose; the battery must be seized before it could be discharged.

"On!" cried Manangani, addressing himself to Martin Paz.

But the young Indian had just stooped and no longer heard him, for an Indian had whispered these words in his ear:

"They are pillaging the house of Don Vegal, perhaps assassinating him!"

At these words Martin Paz recoiled. Manangani seized him by the arm; but, repulsing him with a vigorous hand, the Indian darted toward the square.

"Traitor! infamous traitor!" exclaimed Manangani, discharging his pistols at Martin Paz.

At this moment the cannons were fired, and the grape swept the Indians on the steps.

"This way, brethren," cried Martin Paz, and a few fugitives, his devoted companions, joined him; with this little company he could make his way through the soldiers.

This flight had all the consequences of treason; the Indians believed themselves abandoned by their chief. Manangani in vain attempted to bring them back to the combat; a rapid *fusillade* sent among them a shower of balls; thenceforth it was no longer possible to rally them; the confusion was at its height and the rout complete. The flames which arose in certain quarters attracted some fugitives to pillage; but the conquering soldiers pursued them with the sword, and killed a great number without mercy.

Meanwhile, Martin Paz had gained the house of Don Vegal; it was the theatre of a bloody struggle, headed by the Sambo himself; he had a double interest in being there; while contending with the Spanish noblemen, he wished to seize Sarah, as a pledge of the fidelity of his son.

On seeing Martin Paz return, he no longer doubted his treason, and turned his brethren against him.

The overthrown gate and walls of the court revealed Don Vegal, sword in hand, surrounded by his faithful servants, and contending with an invading mass. This man's courage and pride were sublime; he was the first to present himself to mortal blows, and his formidable arm had surrounded him with corpses.

But what could be done against this crowd of Indians, which was then increasing with all the conquered of the Plaza-Mayor. Don Vegal felt that his defenders were becoming exhausted, and nothing remained for him but death, when Martin Paz arrived, rapid as the thunderbolt, charged the aggressors from behind, forced them to turn against him, and, amid balls, poignard- strokes and maledictions, reached Don Vegal, to whom he made a rampart of his body. Courage revived in the hearts of the besieged.

"Well done, my son, well done!" said Don Vegal to Martin Paz, pressing his hand.

But the young Indian was gloomy.

"Well done! Martin Paz," exclaimed another voice which went to his very soul; he recognized Sarah, and his arm traced a bloody circle around him.

The company of Sambo gave way in its turn. Twenty times had this modern Brutus directed his blows against his son, without being able to reach him, and twenty times Martin had turned away the weapon about to strike his father.

Suddenly the ferocious Manangani, covered with blood, appeared beside the Sambo.

"Thou hast sworn," said he, "to avenge the treason of a wretch on his kindred, on his friends, on himself. Well, it is time! the soldiers are coming; the mestizo, André Certa, is with them."

"Come then," said the Sambo, with a ferocious laugh: "come then, for our vengeance approaches."

And both abandoned the house of Don Vegal, while their companions were being killed there. They went directly to the company who were arriving. The latter aimed at them; but without being intimidated, the Sambo approached the mestizo.

"You are André Certa," said he; "well, your betrothed is in the house of Don Vegal, and Martin Paz is about to carry her to the mountains."

This said, the Indians disappeared. Thus the Sambo had put face to face two mortal enemies, and, deceived by the presence of Martin Paz in the house of Don Vegal, the soldiers rushed upon the dwelling of the marquis.

André Certa was intoxicated with rage. As soon as he perceived Martin Paz, he rushed upon him.

"Here!" exclaimed the young Indian, and quitting the stone steps which he had so valiantly defended, he joined the mestizo. Meanwhile the companions of Martin Paz were repulsing the soldiers body to body.

Martin Paz had seized André Certa with his powerful hand, and clasped him so closely that the mestizo could not use his pistols. They were there, foot against foot, breast against breast, their faces touched, and their glances mingled in a single gleam; their movements became rapid, even invisible; neither friends nor enemies could approach them; in this terrible embrace respiration failed, both fell. André Certa raised himself above Martin Paz, whose poignard had escaped his grasp. The mestizo raised his arm, but the Indian succeeded in seizing it before it had struck. The moment was horrible. André Certa in vain attempted to disengage himself; Martin Paz, with supernatural strength, turned against the mestizo the poignard and the arm which held it, and plunged it into his heart.

Martin Paz arose all bloody. The place was free, the soldiers flying in every direction. Martin Paz might have conquered had he remained on the Plaza-Mayor. He fell into the arms of Don Vegal.

"To the mountains, my son; flee to the mountains! now I command it."

"Is my enemy indeed dead?" said Martin Paz, returning to the corpse of André Certa.

A man was that moment searching it, and held a pocket-book which he had taken from it. Martin Paz sprang on this man and overthrew him; it was the Jew Samuel.

The Indian picked up the pocket-book, opened it hastily, searched it, uttered a cry of joy, and springing toward the marquis, put in his hand a paper on which were written these words:

"Received of the Señor André Certa the sum of 100,000 piasters; I pledge myself to restore this sum doubled, if Sarah, whom I saved from the shipwreck of the *San-José*, and whom he is about to espouse, is not the daughter and only heir of the Marquis Don Vegal.

"SAMUEL."

"My daughter! my daughter!" exclaimed the Spaniard, and he fell into the arms of Martin Paz, who carried him to the chamber of Sarah.

Alas! the young girl was no longer there; Father Joachim, bathed in his own blood, could articulate only these words:

"The Sambo!—carried off!—toward the river of Madeira!—"

And he fainted.

CHAPTER IX.
THE CATARACTS OF THE MADEIRA.

"On! on!" Martin Paz had exclaimed. And without saying a word, Don Vegal followed the Indian. His daughter!—he must find again his daughter! Mules were brought, prepared for a long journey among the Cordilleras; the two men mounted them, wrapped in their *ponchos*; large gaiters were attached by thongs above their knees; immense stirrups, armed with long spurs, surrounded their feet, and broad-brimmed Guayaquil hats sheltered their heads. Arms filled the holsters of each saddle; a carbine, formidable in the hands of Don Vegal, was suspended at his side. Martin Paz had encircled himself with his lasso, one extremity of which was fixed to the harness of his mule.

The Spaniard and the Indian spurred their horses to their utmost speed. At the moment of leaving the walls of the city they were joined by an Indian equipped like themselves. It was Liberta—Don Vegal recognized him; the faithful servant wished to share in their pursuit.

Martin Paz knew all the plains, all the mountains, which they were to traverse; he knew among what savage tribes, into what desert country the Sambo had conveyed his betrothed. His betrothed! he no longer dared give this name to the daughter of Don Vegal.

"My son," said the latter, "have you any hope in your heart?"

"As much as hatred and tenderness."

"The daughter of the Jew, in becoming my blood, has not ceased to be thine."

"Let us press on!" hastily replied Martin Paz.

On their way the travelers saw a great number of Indians flying to regain their *ranchos* amid the mountains. The defection of Martin Paz had been followed by defeat. If the *émeute* had triumphed in some places, it had received its death-blow at Lima.

The three cavaliers traveled rapidly, having but one idea, one object. They soon buried themselves among the almost impracticable passes of the Cordilleras. Difficult pathways circulated through these reddish masses, planted here and there with cocoanut and pine trees; the cedars, cotton-trees, and aloes were left behind them, with the plains covered with maize and lucerne; some thorny cactuses sometimes pricked their mules, and made them hesitate on the verge of precipices.

It was a difficult task to traverse the Cordilleras during these summer months; the melting of snows beneath the sun of June often made unforeseen cataracts spout from beneath the steps of the traveler; often frightful masses, detaching themselves from the summits of the peaks, were engulfed near them in fathomless abysses!

But they continued their march, fearing neither the hurricane nor the cold of these high solitudes; they traveled day and night, finding neither cities nor dwellings where they might for a moment repose; happy if in some deserted hut they found a mat of *tortora* upon which to extend their wearied limbs, some pieces of meat dried in the sun, some calabashes full of muddy water.

They reached at last the summit of the Andes, 14,000 feet above the level of the sea. There, no more trees, no more vegetation; sometimes an *oso* or *ucuman*, a sort of enormous black bear, came to meet them. Often, during the afternoon, they were enveloped in those formidable storms of the Cordilleras, which raise whirlwinds of snow from the loftiest summits. Don Vegal sometimes paused, unaccustomed to these frightful perils. Martin Paz then supported him in his arms, and sheltered him against the drifting snow. And yet lightnings flashed from the clouds, and thunders broke over these barren peaks, and filled the mountain recesses with their terrific roar.

At this point, the most elevated of the Andes, the travelers were seized with a malady called by the Indians *soroche*, which deprives the most intrepid man of his courage and his strength. A superhuman will is then necessary to keep one from falling motionless on the stones of the road, and being devoured by those immense condors which display above their vast wings! These three men spoke little; each wrapped himself in the silence which these vast deserts inspired.

On the eastern slope of the Cordilleras, they hoped to find traces of their enemies; they therefore traveled on, and were at last descending the chain of mountains; but the Andes are composed of a great number of salient peaks, so that inaccessible precipices were constantly rising before them.

Nevertheless they soon found the trees of inferior levels; the llamas, the vigonias, which feed on the thin grass, announced the neighborhood of men. Sometimes they met *gauchos* conducting their *arias* of mules; and more than one *capataz* (leader of a convoy) exchanged fresh animals for their exhausted ones.

In this manner they reached the immense virgin forests which cover the plains situated between Peru and Brazil; they began thenceforth to recover traces of the captors; and it was in the midst of these inextricable woods that Martin

Paz recovered all his Indian sagacity.

Courage returned to the Spaniard, strength returned to Liberta, when a half-extinct fire and prints of footsteps proved the proximity of their enemies. Martin Paz noted all and studied all, the breaking of the little branches, the nature of the vestiges.

Don Vegal feared lest his unfortunate daughter should have been dragged on foot through the stones and thorns; but the Indian showed him some pebbles strongly imbedded in the earth, which indicated the pressure of an animal's foot; above, branches had been pushed aside in the same direction, which could have been reached only by a person on horseback. The poor father comforted himself and recovered life and hope, and then Martin Paz was so confident, so skillful, so strong, that there were for him neither impassable obstacles nor insurmountable perils.

Nevertheless immense forests contracted the horizon around them, and trees multiplied incessantly before their fatigued eyes.

One evening, while the darkness was gathering beneath the opaque foliage, Martin Paz, Liberta and Don Vegal were compelled by fatigue to stop. They had reached the banks of a river; it was the river Madeira, which the Indian recognized perfectly; immense mangrove trees bent above the sleeping wave and were united to the trees on the opposite shore by capricious *lianes* (vines), on which were balancing the *titipaying* and the *concoulies*.

Had the captors ascended the banks? had they descended the course of the river? had they crossed it in a direct line? Such were the questions with which Martin Paz puzzled himself. He stepped a little aside from his companions, following with infinite difficulty some fugitive tracks; these brought him to a clearing a little less gloomy. Some footsteps indicated that a company of men had, perhaps, crossed the river at this spot, which was the opinion of the Indian, although he found around him no proof of the construction of a canoe; he knew that the Sambo might have cut down some tree in the middle of the forest, and having spoiled it of its bark, made of it a boat, which could have been carried on the arms of men to the shores of the Madeira. Nevertheless, he was still hesitating, when he saw a sort of black mass move near a thicket; he quickly prepared his lasso and made ready for an attack; he advanced a few paces, and perceived an animal lying on the ground, a prey to the final convulsions—it was a mule. The poor, expiring beast had been struck at a distance from the spot whither it had been dragged, leaving long traces of blood on its passage. Martin Paz no longer doubted that the Indians, unable to induce it to cross the river, had killed it with the stroke of a poignard, as a deep wound indicated. From this moment he felt certain of the direction of his enemies; and returned to his companions, who were already uneasy at his long absence.

"To-morrow, perhaps, we shall see the young girl!" said he to them.

"My daughter! Oh! my son! let us set out this instant," said the Spaniard; "I am no longer fatigued, and strength returns with hope—let us go!"

"But we must cross this river, and we cannot lose time in constructing a canoe."

"We will swim across."

"Courage, then, my father! Liberta and myself will sustain you."

All three laid aside their garments, which Martin Paz carried in a bundle upon his head; and all three glided silently into the water, for fear of awakening some of these dangerous *caïmans* so numerous in the rivers of Brazil and Peru.

They arrived safely at the opposite shore: the first care of Martin Paz was to recover traces of the Indians; but in vain did he scrutinize the smallest leaves, the smallest pebbles—he could discover nothing; as the rapid current had carried them down in crossing, he ascended the bank of the river to the spot opposite that where he had found the mule, but nothing indicated the direction taken by the captors. It must have been that these, that their tracks might be entirely lost, had descended the river for several miles, in order to land far from the spot of their embarkation.

Martin Paz, that his companions might not be discouraged, did not communicate to them his fears; he said not even a word to Don Vegal respecting the mule, for fear of saddening him still more with the thought that his daughter must now be dragged through these difficult passes.

When he returned to the Spaniard, he found him asleep—fatigue had prevailed over grief and resolution; Martin Paz was careful not to awaken him; a little sleep might do him much good; but, while he himself watched, resting the head of Don Vegal on his knees and piercing with his quick glances the surrounding shadows, he sent Liberta to seek below on the river some trace which might guide them at the first rays of the sun.

The Indian departed in the direction indicated, gliding like a serpent between the high brush with which the shores were bristling, and the sound of his footsteps was soon lost in the distance.

Thenceforth Martin Paz remained alone amid these gloomy solitudes: the Spaniard was sleeping peacefully; the names of his daughter and the Indian sometimes mingled in his dreams, and alone disturbed the silence of these obscure forests.

The young Indian was not mistaken; the Sambo had descended the Madeira three miles, then had landed with the young girl and his numerous companions, among whom might be numbered Manangani, still covered with hideous wounds.

The company of Sambo had increased during the journey. The Indians of the plains and the mountains had awaited with impatience the triumph of the revolt; on learning the failure of their brethren, they fell a prey to a gloomy despair; hearing that they had been betrayed by Martin Paz, they uttered yells of rage; when they saw that they had a victim to be sacrificed to their anger, they burst forth in cries of joy and followed the company of the old Indian.

They marched thus to the approaching sacrifice, devouring the young girl with sanguinary glances—it was the betrothed, the beloved of Martin Paz whom they were about to put to death; abuse was heaped upon her, and more than once the Sambo, who wished his revenge to be public, with difficulty wrested Sarah from their fury.

The young girl, pale, languishing, was without thought and almost without life amid this frightful horde; she had no longer the sentiment of motion, of will, of existence—she advanced, because bloody hands urged her onward; they might have abandoned her in the midst of these great solitudes—she could not have taken a step to have escaped death. Sometimes the remembrance of her father and of the young Indian passed before her eyes, but like a gleam of lightning bewildering her; then she fell again an inert mass on the neck of the poor mule, whose wounded feet could no longer sustain her. When beyond the river she was compelled to follow her captors on foot, two Indians taking her by the arm dragged her rapidly along, and a trace of blood marked on the sand and dead leaves her painful passage.

But the Sambo was no longer afraid of pursuit; he cared little that this blood betrayed the direction he had taken—he was approaching the termination of his journey, and soon the cataracts which abound in the currents of the great river sent up their deafening clamor.

The numerous company of Indians arrived at a sort of village, composed of a hundred huts, made of reeds interlaced and clay; at their approach, a multitude of women and children darted toward them with loud cries of joy— more than one found there his anxious family—more than one wife missed the father of her children!

These women soon learned the defeat of their party; their sadness was transformed into rage on learning the defection of Martin Paz, and on seeing his betrothed devoted to death.

Sarah remained immovable before these enemies and looked at them with a dim eye; all these hideous faces were making grimaces around her, and the most terrific threats were uttered in her ears—the poor child might have thought herself delivered over to the torturers of the infernal regions.

"Where is my husband?" said one; "it is thou who hast caused him to be killed!"

"And my brother, who will never again return to the cabin—what hast thou done with him? Death! death! Let each of us have a piece of her flesh! let each of us have a pain to make her suffer! Death! death!"

And these women, with dishevelled hair, brandishing knives, waving flaming brands, bearing enormous stones, approached the young girl, surrounded her, pressed her, crushed her.

"Back!" cried the Sambo, "back! and let all await the decision of their chiefs! This girl must disarm the anger of the Great Spirit, which has rested upon our arms; and she shall not serve for private revenge alone!"

The women obeyed the words of the old Indian, casting frightful glances on the young girl; the latter, covered with blood, remained extended on the pebbly shore.

Above this village, plunges, from a height of more than a hundred feet, a foaming cataract, which breaks against sharp rocks; the Madeira, contracted into a deep bed, precipitates this dense mass of water with frightful rapidity; a cloud of mist is eternally suspended above this torrent, whose fall sends its formidable and thundering roar afar.

It was in the midst of this foaming tempest that the unfortunate young girl was destined to die; at the first rays of the sun, exposed in a bark canoe above the cataract, she was to be precipitated with the mass of waters on the rude rocks against which the Madeira broke.

So the council of chiefs had decided; and they had delayed until the morrow the punishment of their victim, to give her a night of anguish, of torment, and of terror.

When the sentence was made known, cries of joy welcomed it, and a furious delirium seized the Indians.

It was a night of orgies—a night of blood and of horror; brandy increased the excitement of these wild natives; dances, accompanied with perpetual yells, surrounded the young girl, and wound their fantastic chains about the stake to which she was fastened. Sometimes the circle narrowed, and enlaced her in its furious whirls: the Indians ran through the uncultivated fields, brandishing blazing pine-branches, and surrounding the victim with light.

And it was thus until sunrise, and worse yet when its first rays illuminated the scene. The young girl was detached from the stake, and a hundred arms were stretched out to drag her to execution, when the name of Martin Paz involuntarily escaped her lips, and cries of hatred and of vengeance responded.

It was necessary to climb by steep paths the immense pile of rocks which led to the upper level of the river, and the victim arrived there all bloody; a canoe of bark awaited her a hundred paces above the fall; she was deposited in it, and fastened by bonds which entered her flesh.

"Vengeance and death!" exclaimed the whole tribe, with one voice.

The canoe was hurried on with increasing rapidity and began to whirl.

Suddenly a man appeared on the opposite shore— It is Martin Paz! Beside him, are Don Vegal and Liberta.

"My daughter! my daughter!" exclaims the father, kneeling on the shore.

"My father!" replied Sarah, raising herself up with superhuman strength.

The scene was indescribable. The canoe was rapidly hastening to the cataract, in whose foam it was already enveloped.

Martin Paz, standing on a rock, balanced his lasso which whistled around his head. At the instant the boat was about to be precipitated, the long leathern thong unfolded from above the head of the Indian, and surrounded the canoe with its noose.

"My daughter! my daughter!" exclaimed Don Vegal.

"My betrothed! my beloved!" cried Martin Paz.

"Death!" yelled the savage multitude.

Meanwhile Martin Paz redoubles his efforts; the canoe remains suspended over the abyss; the current cannot prevail over the strength of the young Indian; the canoe is drawn to him; the enemies are far on the opposite shore; the young girl is saved.

Suddenly an arrow whistles through the air, and pierces the heart of Martin Paz. He falls forward in the bark of the victim; and, re-descending the current of the river in her arms, is engulfed with Sarah in the vortex of the cataract.

A yell of triumph is heard above the sound of the torrent.

Liberta bore off the Spaniard amid a cloud of arrows, and disappeared with him.

Don Vegal regained Lima, where he died with grief and exhaustion.

The Sambo, who remained among his sanguinary tribes, was never heard of more.

The Jew Samuel kept the hundred thousand piasters he had received, and continued his usuries at the expense of the Limanian nobles.

Martin Paz and Sarah were, in their brief and final re-union, betrothed for eternity.